Brett turned on her
"How dare you judge me—"

Knowing that his next words would be to tell her she was fired, Emma decided she might as well go out with flags flying. "It's time someone told you the truth. Cindy's sick with love for you, yet for all the notice you take of her, you might as well be as dead as your wife!"

Lunging for her, he shook her furiously, then stopped, his hands shaking, his face pale. "I'm sorry. I never lose my temper but you..."

"I'd no right to say what I did," Emma murmured as he carried her to a chair.

"You care," he muttered. "That gives you the right. And I also owe you an explanation."

Emma knew if she had any sense she'd walk out and not stop until she'd put an ocean between herself and this man. But something held her where she was....

"Your mother was very beautiful," Brett said

ROBERTA LEIGH wrote her first book at the age of nineteen and since then has written more than seventy romance novels, as well as many books and film series for children. She has also been an editor of a women's magazine and produced a teen magazine, but writing romance fiction remains one of her greatest joys. She lives in Hampstead, London, and has one son.

Books by Roberta Leigh

LOVE WATCH

HARLEQUIN PRESENTS

HARLEQUIN ROMANCE

Don't miss any of our special offers. Write to us at the following address for information on our newest releases.

Harlequin Reader Service
901 Fuhrmann Blvd., P.O. Box 1397, Buffalo, NY 14240
Canadian address: P.O. Box 603,
Fort Erie, Ont. L2A 5X3

ROBERTA LEIGH

a racy affair

Harlequin Books

TORONTO • NEW YORK • LONDON
AMSTERDAM • PARIS • SYDNEY • HAMBURG
STOCKHOLM • ATHENS • TOKYO • MILAN

Harlequin Presents first edition November 1987
ISBN 0-373-11026-X

Original hardcover edition published in 1987
by Mills & Boon Limited

CHAPTER ONE

As the Brazilian Airlines jet rose from the runway and Emma Fielding saw Heathrow airport spread out below her, she knew a moment of blind panic. She had been crazy to accept a job on the other side of the world, working for a man she'd never met. And crazier still when she knew him to be a female-scalp collector like Brett Adams!

She glanced round her and, seeing the passengers settling back and relaxing, felt her tension ease. After all, what did it matter how far she was from England? She had a return ticket in her purse and could always come home if things didn't work out. Except that home wouldn't be the same now her mother was dead—which was exactly why Charles Walpole, their family doctor and friend, had suggested she take a term's absence from nursery school, and have a complete change of scene.

'You worked like a Trojan keeping up your job and looking after your mother,' was the way he had broached it, 'and now it's time you started looking after yourself.'

'And do what?' she had asked despondently.

'How do you fancy spending the winter in sunny Brazil?'

'I've as much chance of that as a pig flying!'

'Any animal can fly if you put it on a plane!'

'Meaning?'

'That there's an ideal post going in a seaside resort a few hours from Rio.'

5

'There has to be a snag!'

'There isn't one. All you have to do is be governess to a seven year-old girl until her father sends her to boarding-school in England after Easter.'

'How did you hear of the position?' Emma had asked.

'The father is the son of an old friend of mine from Yorkshire, and he happened to mention it when I rang him for a chat.'

'I don't believe in sending a seven-year-old to boarding-school,' Emma had stated.

'Nor do I. But in Cindy's case it's the best solution. She hasn't a mother, and the alternative is for her father to take her with him on his travels—which he's done from time to time, though I gather it's made her run completely wild.'

'That has nothing to do with travel,' Emma had commented. 'It comes from lack of discipline.'

Her silver-grey eyes had gleamed with disapproval. Facially they were her best feature, fringed by thick lashes several shades darker than the toffee-coloured hair, which fell heavy and shining to her shoulders. Her skin had a pearly translucence that neither sun nor icy wind could mar, and her delicate bone structure brought to mind the fey creatures in Victorian children's books, who flitted through trees in flower-filled gardens. Yet although Emma outwardly fitted the bill, she was a determined and intelligent girl underneath, and it was this mixture of the fey and the fiery that men found so attractive.

Not that she'd had much time for men since leaving college, for her mother's illness had started then, and Emma had preferred to stay at home with her, rather than socialise. But all that was in the past. She was an orphan—what a lonely word it was—and had to build a new life for herself.

In all honesty, the thought of remaining at the

nursery school in her home village didn't give her any surge of joy, though she was level-headed enough to know she was not in the mood to take on a big city with its problems of accommodation and a faster way of life. Because of this, a temporary job in Brazil seemed just what the doctor had ordered—and, best of all, the doctor *had* ordered it!

'Who exactly will I be working for?' she had asked, rolling down the sleeves of her dress to hide arms that had become too thin.

'Brett Adams.'

'The racing driver?'

'Yes.'

Emma had frowned. This put a whole new complexion on the job. Celebrities had never been her scene, and this one in particular, whose name hit the headlines with the frequency of Princess Diana's, was the kind from whom she'd run a mile.

'It's no good, I'm afraid. I couldn't work for him. He's an unmitigated chauvinist. I once heard him give a radio interview and I nearly blew a gasket!'

'You'll be looking after his daughter, not him. Anyway, if you're such a liberated female, why let a mere male put you off a cushy little job in the sun that can only do you the world of good?'

It was a powerful argument, and it had won the day. Besides, coping with one seven-year-old instead of a dozen four-year-olds sounded like heaven!

Reading her expression correctly, Charles Walpole had pressed home the advantages. 'A bit of cosseting in a luxurious home is exactly what you need to get your strength back. And you'll barely see Brett, if that's what's worrying you. He races—literally and metaphorically—all round the world. Drop him a line with your qualifications. It's my bet he'll want you there as soon as possible.'

The good doctor's bet had been justified, and on a

particularly cold night in October, with early frost sprinkling the ground, Emma had found herself— after hurried preparations—winging her way to Rio de Janeiro, and nervously wondering what awaited her when the jet touched down.

But no amount of imagery prepared her for the beauty of their approach into Galileo airport, the vividness of the madonna-blue sky and sunshine, the blast of heat and humidity that greeted her as she emerged from the aircraft. Enraptured, she stared at the magnificent bulk of the Sugar Loaf Mountain where the huge, white statue of Christ—enormous even from a distance—gave its benediction to the city.

Bemused, Emma followed the crowd into the terminal building. It was filled with a diversity of people of every imaginable skin tone, from white to bronze to yellow to black—and all around her the soft, hissing sound of Portuguese.

But she had little time to stop and stare, for she had to catch an immediate onward flight that would take her five hundred miles down the coast to the town of Embira, where she would be met and driven another five miles to the village of Mertola, where Brett Adams had built his home and practice-track.

Her first sight of the aircraft that was to take her on the second leg of her journey almost made Emma turn tail and run. It looked like a sewing machine with wings! Too imaginative to be the most sanguine of air travellers, she had no faith whatever in this little aircraft bobbing about in the sky, although none of the other passengers seemed concerned as they mounted the steps, disposed of their hand luggage and made themselves comfortable in the small interior.

Well, if Brazilians could do it, so could she, Emma thought. After all, didn't she come from the country of the stiff upper lip? Biting her lower one to still its trembling, she took her place and fastened her seat belt.

Dark-haired, olive-skinned cabin staff moved quickly along the aisles to ensure everyone was settled. Engines whined, propellers whirred, and Emma's terror mounted as the plane moved bumpily along the runway, then increased both speed and sound as it raced forward, seeming to go to the very edge of the airfield before lifting like a wounded bird into the sky.

For a long while she clutched at the arm rests, as though by her very fingers she could keep the plane airborne, and only when her hands grew numb did she tentatively put them on her lap. But the plane proceeded merrily on its way, and soon she allowed herself to relax.

A stewardess offered her coffee and Emma accepted a cup, glad it was strong. She had barely slept since leaving London, and needed the caffeine to keep her awake when she met her new empoyer!

By now the calm atmosphere on the plane had restored her confidence, and she peered through the window. They were flying low, and instead of clouds—as on her long haul—she had a panoramic view of the scenery: tree-covered mountains, golden beaches, and bays dotted with tiny, palm fringed islands.

The airport at Embira reminded her of one in an old Spanish film she had seen many years ago, with its solitary runway and single-storeyed concrete building which most passengers ignored, waiting by the plane for their luggage to be handed down to them, before walking directly out.

Within moments Emma found herself alone in the arrivals hall. No one was there to meet her and it was as hot as Hades, the noisy air conditioning chattering

heatedly to itself, and making no difference to the
blazing temperature.

Sitting in a blue plastic chair, she waited patiently,
and only when half an hour had ticked by did she go
over to the counter which served as ticket seller,
luggage check and information centre, to ask if
anyone had left a message for her.

No one had, nor was there another plane due in
from Rio. Well, at least that lessened the confusion,
for Brett Adams wasn't likely to meet the wrong one!
Swallowing her irritation—she'd travelled practically
half-way round the world, and he only had to go
a few miles—she acknowledged she found his
unpunctuality rude in the extreme.

Returning to her seat, she caught sight of herself in
a mirrored wall. Heavens! What she'd give for a bath
and a change into something cooler. Picking up her
hand luggage, she went into the cloakroom, splashed
water on her sweaty face, and ran a comb through
her hair. That was better. Like giving a quick lick of
paint to a house you wanted to sell! she thought
humorously. Not that she cared to sell herself to
Brett Adams. She was here solely to teach the three
rs to his daughter.

Still, eyeing her pink, cotton-knit suit, she was
sorry she had worn it. It had stood up well to the
rigours of travel, but it tended to cling to her figure,
and pink—while giving colour to her pearly skin—
made her look rather young to be a governess.

Refusing to let her spirits droop, she returned to
the hall. Hardly had she resettled herself when a tall,
slim man in his early thirties came through the
entrance, looked around, then walked directly across
to her. As he drew nearer, she saw he was lightly
tanned and that his large, generous mouth turned up
at the corners in a smile that matched the humour in
his pale blue eyes.

'Miss Fielding?' At Emma's nod, he engulfed her hand in his large one. 'I guessed it was you from your pale skin! Sorry to keep you waiting—I was held up. I hope you'll forgive me?'

'Of course.' She'd forgive him anything now he was here!

He summoned a porter to carry her luggage, then guided her out to his car. Anticipating something sporty, she was surprised to see a dusty grey station wagon. But then Mr Adams himself had surprised her, for he was nowhere near the forceful man she had imagined. He was casual to the point of boyishness, and she felt totally at ease with him. If Cindy was as nice as her father seemed, these next few months should be more of a vacation than a job!

Soon they were driving along the main road, and once again Emma glanced at the man beside her. In profile he looked even younger than full face, partly due to his snub nose and the way his hair curled round his ears. In no sense could he be considered handsome, though he was undeniably attractive.

Sensing her watching him, he turned and smiled. 'How was your flight?'

'Excellent. I was only sorry I didn't have time to see more of Rio.'

'Maybe you will on your way back home—or perhaps I can take you there myself one weekend?'

'Thank you, but I wouldn't want you to go to any trouble,' she replied, vaguely disquieted.

'A pretty girl is the kind of trouble I like!'

Her disquiet intensified. 'I'm sure you know many girls prettier than me,' she said. 'In your profession you must be a prime target for celebrity-struck females!'

'In my profession?' He sounded surprised, then unexpectedly chuckled. 'Hey, I'm not Brett Adams! I'm Bill Sanderson—the boss's general factotum.'

'Oh!' Emma was relieved, yet at the same time dismayed, for the ordeal of meeting her new employer still loomed ahead of her.

'That was a very significant "oh",' Bill Sanderson grinned, 'but I'm used to it.'

'Used to what?'

'Having a girl look disappointed when she discovers I'm not Brett. Fame does wonders for a man's sex appeal!'

'It would turn me off,' Emma assured him.

'That's the nicest thing you could have said to me. I can see you're going to be a frank and entertaining addition to our household! I hope you'll find it enjoyable too.'

'I'm not too sure,' Emma confessed. 'To be honest, I was so worried at working for a celebrity I almost didn't take the job.'

'You're having me on! Girls fall over themselves to work for Brett.'

'That's what worried me!'

'Forget the gossip.'

'Isn't it true, then?'

'Let's say it's exaggerated. Sure the boss likes women—what normal man doesn't? But he steers clear of those who work for him. He also spends ninety per cent of his time on the race track, and that's both mentally and physically exhausting. So all those carousing nights you've read about should be divided by ten and ten again!'

Emma took the rebuke in good humour, and seeing the village of Mertola ahead of them, deemed it wiser to talk of something else. 'Have we far to go?'

'We're nearly there. The estate's a few miles north.'

Emma dabbed away the perspiration trickling down her face. 'Is it always so hot here?'

'This is considered cool!' Bill smiled. 'But you'll soon get used to it.'

'I hope so.' She looked through the window at the coastline: wide, silver sand beaches edged by blue-grey sea and foam-crested waves. 'Is it safe for bathing?'

'In the bath or pool only! There are strong undercurrents and you could easily get carried out to sea. But the boss has his own pool and we're all free to use it.'

'Is this Mr Adams's permanent home? I'm sorry to ask so many questions but I know hardly anything about him.'

'Except what you read!' came the teasing rejoinder. 'But no, his home proper is in Yorkshire, where the Adams cars are made. Their sales have multiplied a hundredfold since Brett started racing them. He's marvellous publicity for the company.'

'Couldn't he get publicity less dangerously?'

'Don't let Brett hear you say that,' Bill warned. 'He's got a thing about nervous women.'

'What else should I watch out for?' she asked. 'I don't want to annoy him.'

'Well, he doesn't like females who come on too strong. Not that it stops them, mind you! Also, he has no patience with ditherers, and he doesn't suffer fools.'

'He sound exactly like every other man!' Emma commented, and Bill chuckled.

'Not quite,' he replied. 'But I'll leave you to find out the difference for yourself!'

Easing his foot off the accelerator, Bill swung the car between two gate posts and proceeded along a curving driveway. On either side grew lush vegetation—magnificent greenery, brillant-coloured flowers, their blooms so large they looked artificial— and brightly feathered birds shrieked happily in the tall trees, where frond-like leaves drooped in the motionless air.

A quarter of a mile further on, around another bend, Emma had her first sight of a sprawling grey stone *hacienda*, with a wide wooden veranda supported by slender columns encircling the entire ground floor.

'How lovely!' she murmured. 'It exactly suits the setting.'

'Brett designed it himself.'

An engine whined in the distance and she tilted her head. 'That sounds like a racing car.'

'His new baby!' came the reply. 'The Adams Three. It only arrived this week, and he's just started testing it.'

'What does this mean? I'm so ignorant about racing, there's no point my pretending otherwise.'

'Don't ever pretend with the boss,' came the instant reply. 'That's something else to remember. He hates anyone claiming they know about the sport when they don't.' The throb of an engine came again, reminding Bill of her question. 'Brett tests the cars on the track—it runs round the north and west of the estate—and if they're sluggish or don't stand up to the pounding he gives them, then it's either back to the drawing board or back to the engineers.'

'You mean the cars are returned to England?'

'Sometimes. But frequently they're worked on here.'

'Sounds an expensive business,' Emma murmured as they stopped outside the house.

'You can say that again!' Hand on the wheel, Bill turned to her, 'One more thing. Don't criticise racing. That really drives him spare. As I said, it's his whole life.'

'Where does his daughter fit in?' Emma couldn't help asking.

For an instant Bill looked blank. Then he got the drift of the question and frowned. 'She's part of his life too, of course. But I was talking about his passion—and that's reserved for cars.'

'On which subject I'll stay mute,' Emma assured him. 'I'm here to look after Mr Adams's daughter—only.'

'Glad to hear it. I wish the others had thought the same.'

'Others?'

'The last four governesses. The boss fired them because they were more interested in caring for him!'

'He won't have that problem with me,' Emma said tartly, following Bill to the front door. 'I'm looking forward to meeting Cindy,' she went on, trying to hide her nervousness. 'Where is she?'

'Hiding, I imagine. She's anti-governess at the moment. She couldn't stand the last two.'

Emma entered the house, her spirits warming as she took in the large square hall with its terracotta-tiled floor and hand-carved console table, on which stood an enormous pottery vase filled with red poppies.

'How gorgeous!' she exclaimed.

Bill looked pleased. 'Hang on a minute while I fetch your luggage,'

He went out again and Emma heard him speaking to someone.

'Brett's coming up the drive,' Bill said, re-entering the hall with her cases. 'I can't wait to see his face when he meets you. You're quite different from what he expected.'

'What do you mean?' Alarm shot through her.

'I'll let him tell you himself.'

Before she could protest, he moved to one side, giving Emma her first glimpse of the man for whom she was going to work.

CHAPTER TWO

AT first glance, Brett Adams looked a physically perfect and perfectly handsome specimen of manhood.

Standing well over six feet tall, he had long legs and narrow hips encased in blue cotton slacks the same shade as the shirt pulled across his wide sloping shoulders, the open collar revealing a strongly-corded neck, as deeply bronzed as the well-muscled arms. His face was narrow, with high cheekbones, and he had a thin, somewhat supercilious nose counterbalanced by a beautifully shaped mouth, held now in a disapproving line.

Disapproval was also apparent in the sherry-brown eyes regarding her, their colour the same as the thick layered hair, which, as he moved into the light she couldn't help noticing, held definite mahogany glints, and drew attention to the strongly shaped head. A sign of short temper? she wondered, and became aware of a tension about him.

'Miss Fielding?'

His voice was as deep and dynamic as his looks, as he gripped her hand with a well-controlled movement.

'You're younger than I expected,' he went on. 'I assumed you'd be in your thirties.'

She was dismayed. 'Dr Walpole told you that?'

'No, no. It's the impression I got from your letter, apart from your name—Emma Constance Fielding. Hardly what one associates with a teenager!' His glance raked her. 'How old are you, anyway—eighteen?'

'Twenty-three.' Her head lifted sharply. 'And everything in my curriculum vitae is true. I'm a qualified nursery school teacher, experienced in looking after young children.'

'Your experience will certainly be put to the test with Cindy,' he said without smiling. 'I doubt you'll be able to control her.'

'Do you always pre-judge a situation, Mr Adams?'

Eyes stared at her from beneath lowered eyebrows, and Emma realised he was not used to having his statements questioned. But then she didn't like his tone and saw no reason to tolerate rudeness. After all, politeness cost nothing.

'I assume you're capable of introducing Cindy to the three rs,' he went on, ignoring her question.

'That's part of what I'm trained for.'

'Part?' One well-defined eyebrow lifted. 'What else can you do?'

'Cope with difficult children, and recognise what causes certain behaviour. Tantrums can be a sign of boredom, while——'

'OK, Miss Fielding, you've made your point. But you'll need all your expertise when dealing with my daughter. She's been through five governesses in the past two years—which I think speaks for itself.'

'I was under the impression they left because of you, not your daughter,' Emma blurted out, then went scarlet as she saw her employer fling an angry glance at Bill Gibbons. 'I'm sorry,' she apologised. 'That was tactless of me.'

'Erroneous too,' he said icily. 'My behaviour had nothing to do with their departures.'

'I know.' Emma was mortified with herself. 'And— and I just want to say you won't have that problem with me.'

She received a look that was distinctly derisive, and she had to resist the urge to turn and walk out.

Indeed, had this meeting taken place in England, she would have left after the first handshake!

'Bill, take Miss Fielding to meet Cindy,' came the command.

'Wouldn't it be better if you introduced me to your daughter yourself?' Emma suggested.

'I don't see why. She knows I'm extremely busy. That's why you're here. To keep her happy and out of my way.' Turning on his heel he started across the hall. Then he stopped and glanced over his shoulder. 'By the way, you'll take your meals with Cindy, except for Sundays. If I'm around that day, you both lunch with me.'

'How nice,' Emma said tonelessly.

The man's mouth tightened, but without a word he strode into the room opposite her and closed the door behind him.

'I've known better beginnings,' Bill murmured. 'You're quite a fire-cracker, aren't you?'

'Only when someone lights the match!' Emma gave a rueful sigh. 'It was pretty awful, I agree. But he was so gratuitously rude the instant he saw me I lost my temper.'

'Try to see if from his angle. He was expecting a mature woman and in came a sprite!' Pale eyes roamed her. 'Are you really twenty-three?'

'I've my passport to prove it.' She went to open her purse but the amused shake of his head stopped her, and instead she bent to pick up her smallest case.

'Leave it,' Bill ordered. 'One of the houseboys will take them up.'

'Maybe it might be wiser for me to leave most of my luggage down here, ready for a smart departure!'

Bill chuckled. 'It wasn't as bad as that. By tomorrow Brett will have forgotten the whole thing.'

Not sure she could say the same for herself, Emma said bluntly, 'Is he always so short-tempered?'

'Sometimes he's worse! Hey, don't look so horrified—I was kidding! But your arrival wasn't exactly opportune. He's in a foul mood today because the car's giving trouble. We'll have to make several modifications and that will lose him practice hours.' Bill moved towards the stairs. 'Come on, let's go find Cindy.'

Emma followed him up the shallow flight of stairs to the first floor, and along a wide corridor with rooms leading off both sides. The little girl's suite was at the end, and consisted of an enormous day nursery which opened into an equally large bedroom with its own bathroom. There was no sign of Cindy, and though Bill called her, she did not appear.

'She must be hiding,' he said. 'I'll ask the servants to look for her.'

A slight movement behind one of the curtains caught Emma's eye but she pretended not to see it.

'I'd rather you didn't right now,' she said to Bill with a wink. 'I don't particularly want to see her yet,'

He immediately cottoned on and gave a conspiratorial grin. 'In that case, I'll push off,'

'You haven't shown me my room!'

'So I haven't.'

Grimacing at his forgetfulness, he led her the few yards to a room overlooking the swimming pool. It was simply furnished with a low divan, fitted cupboards and dressing table. The polished floor was scattered with bright, hand-woven rugs, and in the far corner stood a rocking chair, beautifully carved in a wood she had never seen before.

Emma examined it with interest. 'What's it called?'

'Brazilwood. 'It's used a great deal here.'

'I know so little about this country,' she confessed.

'That's true of most visitors. But once they've been

here, they're always keen to return. It has everything, you know. Masses of space, magnificent scenery and wonderful flora and fauna.'

'You sound like a travel guide,' she smiled.

'Travelling's my passion.' Bill went to the door. 'About your meals. I know Brett expects you to have breakfast and lunch with Cindy, but he didn't mean for you to have supper with her as well.'

'He certainly didn't suggest I dine with him!'

'I realise that,' Bill coloured. 'What I meant was that you could dine with me and the other chaps, if you like. I often go out for a meal too, and I'd be delighted to take you with me. In fact, if you're free this evening we can——'

'Not tonight, thanks. I want to meet Cindy as soon as I can, and also catch up on my sleep.'

'It was quick of you to guess she was behind the curtain.'

'Not really. She wanted to annoy me, and half the fun of doing so is to be able to see that your ploy is working. That's why I knew she wouldn't be far away.'

'And why you pretended you didn't care whether you saw her or not?'

'Exactly. If she thinks I'm disinterested, she'll come looking for me.'

'And if she doesn't?'

'Then I'll wander around, relax a bit and have an early night. By morning, her curiosity will have got the better of her.'

Bill laughed. 'Poor Cindy. I've an idea she's met her match in you.'

'No "may" about it. She has!'

Grinning, Bill left her, and Emma set about unpacking.

She had started on her second suitcase when the door burst open and a mutinous seven-year-old rushed in. Her expression was so like that of the mahogany-haired man had who had glared at Emma half an hour ago that she was hard put not to laugh. But she stopped herself in time and stared silently at her visitor.

She was tall for her age, with gangling arms and legs. Her face was thin, with a snub nose and pointed chin, and her hair was pulled tightly back into two scraggy plaits. But it was the same deep chestnut as her father's. Her eyes were like his too: sherry-brown and slanting upwards. If first impressions were anything to go by, they even had similar temperaments, for she gave every evidence of being highly spoiled.

'So you're my new governess,' Cindy piped in a high voice. 'You won't be staying long!'

Emma smiled blandly and held out her hand. 'Hello, Cindy. Yes, I'm Emma Fielding.'

'I'll call you Emma. I called all my governesses by their first name.'

The tone of the statement showed the child was waiting for her to protest, but Emma merely nodded aggreeably.

'That's fine with me. Using first names is much friendlier I think, and I hope we will be friends.'

Cindy tossed her head. 'Daddy gave me your letter to read,' she went on, as if implying there were no secrets between father and daughter. 'He said if I don't like you, he'll send you away.'

'How clever of you to read grown-up writing,' Emma replied, ignoring the last part of the remark. 'Most children of your age can only manage print.'

'I'm the best reader in the world,' Cindy bridled.

'I'm glad to hear it. Would you like to show me?'

'I don't have lessons after four o'clock, so you can't boss me around until tomorrow.'

'I don't boss anyone around at any time, Cindy.'

'All governesses are bossy.'

'You'll soon find out I'm not.'

Emma resumed her unpacking, aware of the child's gaze as she stood scuffling the rug nervously with one small foot, and tugging at one of her skimpy plaits. For all her bravado, Cindy was obviously nothing more than an insecure seven-year-old.

'I brought you this,' Emma said casually, placing a package on the bed.

'Why? You don't know me.'

'It's a getting-to-know-you present.'

'I haven't got one for you.'

'That doesn't matter. See if you like it.'

Emma carried a pile of clothes over to the wardrobe. Behind her, she heard paper tearing. Then there was a gasp, followed by silence. Turning casually, she saw Cindy staring open-mouthed at a tiny sewing machine.

'Is it a toy?' the child managed to say.

'Sort of. But it really works. I'll show you later on.'

'What can it make?'

'Lots of things. Dresses for your dolls and——'

'I don't play with dolls. I like cars and boats.'

'I see.'

And Emma did. One didn't have to be psychologist to understand the reason for Cindy's preference. She'd like anything that made her feel closer to her father.

'There are lots of other things we can make,' Emma said. 'Table mats, a nightdress for you, a pyjama case for your father."

'Daddy doesn't wear pyjamas. He says——'

'Or a toilet bag,' Emma went on hastily. 'I brought some material with me and I'll cut it out for you tomorrow.'

'Do it today.'

'I'm too tired. I've had a long journey and I'm going to have a bath and a rest.'

Cindy scowled, but Emma ignored it and placed some books on the table beside her bed.

'Do you live in England?' the child asked.

'Yes. In a village outside London.'

'With your mummy and daddy?'

'No. They're both dead.' Emma kept her tone casual, unwilling to bring any of her own emotions into Cindy's life.

'I've only got my daddy,' the little girl declared, 'and he takes me with him all over the world.'

The statement was so vehement, Emma doubted its truth.

'I don't think I'd like to travel around too much,' she said carefully. 'It wouldn't give me a chance to make friends.'

'I don't want friends. I've got my daddy. He's very unhappy if I'm not with him.'

Emma made a mental note to ask Bill whether her employer did, in fact, take Cindy with him on all his trips. A man who couldn't spare the time to introduce a new governess to his daughter wasn't the type to want her company on his travels. The child was plainly living in a fantasy world, believing what she wanted to believe.

'What time do you have supper?' she asked to change the subject.

'Whenever I like. And it isn't supper, it's proper dinner.'

'I think you should have your main meal at lunchtime, and something lighter in the evening.'

Cindy shook her head. 'I always eat at the same time as my daddy.'

'Together?' Emma asked, curious to see how far the child would go with her pretence.

'Yes. 'Cept when he's busy and—and I eat by myself.'

The pathos behind this remark touched Emma, but she was careful not to show it.

'I still think it's better for you to have your main meal at lunchtime,' she said firmly, and went to run a bath.

She had almost finished undressing when Cindy appeared in the doorway.

'Wait in the bedroom, please, Cindy.'

'Why? I used to watch my last two governesses. They wore bikinis during the day and we had all our lessons in the garden so we could sunbathe at the same time.'

For Brett Adams's benefit, no doubt, Emma thought. No wonder he's cynical about the women who've worked for him!

'Well, I'm different,' she said aloud. 'I prefer to undress in private, and I don't think you can concentrate on lessons if you're sitting in a bikini in the sunshine.'

'You're a spoilsport,' came the mutinous response.

'I'm afraid I am,' Emma said cheerfully, and catching Cindy by the hand, pushed her gently out the door.

'I don't want to see you undressed, anyway,' Cindy muttered. 'You're old and ugly—not like the others!'

Emma bolted the door. Cindy was unquestionably going to pose a problem. She liked her own way, and if she couldn't get it, would resort to tantrums. Not that this would help her, Emma vowed grimly. If she couldn't handle a naughty seven-year-old she'd give up teaching and become a plumber!

Sliding into the warm water, she slowly felt herself relax. She would need to be firm and kind with the child. She was clearly disturbed by her father's indifference to her, and her governesses' interest in Brett and lack of interest in their charge could only have added to her feelings of rejection.

Drying herself and putting on a housecoat, Emma returned to the bedroom. Cindy had gone, and she lay on the bed watching the sunlight on the ceiling and listening to the rustle of the trees outside.

'I think you've let me in for more than I bargained for, Dr Walpole,' she murmured to herself. 'A class of toddlers would be a doddle compared with this seven-year-old monster!'

Upon which thought she turned her head into the pillow and fell asleep.

Emma was awoken from a deep sleep by a knock on the door.

'Come in,' she called, yawning and rubbing her eyes.

A slender, dark-skinned girl in a blue dress and white apron came in with a pot of coffee and a plate of delicious-looking cakes, thick with raisins and nuts.

'How gorgeous!' Emma exclaimed, then tried it out in Portuguese. *"Que bonito."*

The girl beamed. *"Pensava que tinhas fome."*

This was beyond Emma's grasp, and she smiled and shook her head. *"Não comprendo."*

'No matter. Mr Gibbons theenk you hungry, so we bring food,' the maid replied in sing-song English.

'That's very kind of you, er—I'm afraid I don't know your name.'

'Is Maria.'

'Have you worked here long, Maria?'

'*Quatro*—four years.'

'Then you knew Cindy's mother?'

'Yes.' The girl's smile vanished, and averting her head, she scurried out.

Emma's curiosity was instantly aroused, and she wondered in what circumstances the woman had died and now happy the marriage had been. Pity she hadn't thought to ask Dr Walpole.

Most important, though, was to find out what Cindy's relationship had been with her mother. Losing a parent at such a young age was always traumatic, and could explain her emotional dependence on her father. At the best of times such dependence was unhealthy, and in these particular circumstances it could be disastrous. Brett Adams might be fond of his daughter despite his attitude, but Emma was convinced his feelings for her in no way matched hers for him. And if Cindy should ever realise it . . .

Emma sighed. Disinterested though she was in her employer's private life, she'd have better chance of handling the situation if she knew a little more of the background. But she'd have to time her questions carefully and diplomatically if she didn't want to find herself winging back to England!

At six o'clock, changed into a lilac dress that deepened the grey of her eyes, she made her way down to the kitchen.

There was a staff of five, and she introduced herself to them, There was Ana the cook, whose smile was as wide as her girth, and Luisa her assistant, as well as three maids, Maria, whom she had already met, and her two cousins. They all wore blue cotton dresses and greeted her with friendly curiosity, giggling among themselves when she said she'd be staying until Cindy went to boarding-school.

'Many women say same, but all go quickly,' Ana said.

Letting the comment pass, Emma asked her if Cindy could have her main meal at lunchtime, and the cook nodded as she bent to remove a hugh casserole from the oven.

As she placed the heavy iron pot on one of the tiled work surfaces, a delicious meaty aroma filled the air, and Emma sniffed appreciatively.

'Hmm. What is it?'

"Feijoada."

Ana lifted the lid and Emma peered into the steamy interior, seeing a thick, black-bean stew with chunks of assorted meats. She recognised beef and pork and there were also tiny sausages, which were emitting their own garlicky aroma.

'Is this for our supper tonight?' she asked.

'No. Is lamb chops for you an' the little one. Thees for Mr Adams and men. I serve with rice an' slices orange.'

It sounded extremely appetising and Emma, who could have lamb chops any day of the week back at home, made a mental note to ask if she could have Brazilian dishes whenever possible.

Leaving the kitchen, she wandered through the various reception rooms. They were all furnished in dark Brazilwood, colour given by the flowery materials at the windows and covering the settees and armchairs, as well as by the bowls of hibiscus and orchids that stood on every available table.

Yet, though elegant, the house had the atmosphere of a hotel rather than a home, probably because so few personal things were in evidence. A pile of car magazines lay strewn on the coffee table in the main living-room, and a child's bicycle stood incongruously against the wall behind the dining-room door. But there were no photographs or personal mementoes, and she had the impression that her employer had never really settled here but was just passing through.

Still, that was his lifestyle. Here today and gone tomorrow. In more ways than one, she thought with a shiver, recollecting the high mortality rate in his profession. Did he ever consider what would happen to his daughter if he were killed? Maybe that's why he was sending her to boarding-school, so she would lose her attachment to him. Yet no matter what friendships Cindy formed, no one could take the place of her father—even a seemingly uncaring one.

Watch it, Emma warned herself. She was jumping to conclusions on insufficient evidence. Brett Adams was a highly successful man and one couldn't expect him to devote much time to a seven-year-old. Yet not to spare a few minutes to introduce his daughter to her new governess bespoke an attitude that was far from caring.

'There I go again!' Emma muttered, and walked resolutely out of the front door.

The beauty of the tropical garden helped her relax. Lush green lawns—the grass thicker and denser than any she had seen in England—were dotted with palms and monkey-puzzle trees, and beds of gaudily coloured flowers scented warm air filled with bird song.

'How pretty you look among the flowers,' a soft voice said, and she swung round to see Bill. 'Had a good rest?' he enquired.

'Yes, thanks'

'How are you finding Cindy?'

'Difficult but manageable—so far. She wanted to stay with me while I had a bath.'

'Can't say I blame her! So would I.'

Emma blushed. 'I led with the chin on that!'

'You sure did!' He strolled beside her as she continued to walk. 'I hope you and Cindy hit it off. She's a good kid, really. I'm very fond of her.'

'Is her father?'

Bill looked taken aback. 'Of course.'

'How much does he see of her?' Emma persisted. 'I'm not being idly curious, Bill. There's a reason for my question.'

'Brett's a busy man,' came the reply. 'Racing takes him all over the world, and even when he isn't travelling, he's tied up with a mass of things.'

'Such as?'

'Testing engines, working on designs for better ones, developing new prototypes, to say nothing of maintaining a highly visible profile to help sell Adam cars. It's a full-time occupation, believe me, and doesn't leave him much opportunity to be a family man.'

'Most men with busy jobs manage to find some space for their families,' Emma replied. 'Children aren't toys to be taken out of the cupboard to play with when the mood takes you. If that's what he thinks, he shouldn't have had a child in the first place.'

'That's a pretty harsh criticism to level at him,' Bill protested. 'Anyway, Brett wasn't so famous when Cindy was born. It wasn't until his wife died that his career really took off.'

A death wish? Emma wondered, but knew better than to ask. She had already said as much as she dared to Bill.

They came to a small rise, and as they breasted it she gave an exclamation of delight. Below them lay an expanse of grass, and beyond it the flat, grey-blue of an estuary leading to the sea only a quarter of a mile away.

'It's beautiful,' she murmured. 'You could keep a boat here.'

'We do—several in fact. The boathouse is over there, behind that clump of trees. Brett has a motor boat if you fancy water skiing.'

'I suppose he's good at all sports,' she said, thinking sourly that he appeared to have plenty of time for hobbies but none for his daughter.

'He has marvellous co-ordination and stamina,' Bill agreed. 'Which is what you'd expect him to have! But he has a cautious streak too, and never does anything dangerous.'

Emma burst out laughing. 'What's motor racing then? Sport for toddlers?'

'I meant dangerous hobbies,' Bill grinned. 'Racing's his job. And even there he doesn't take chances.'

'Everything about racing is chancy!'

Bill went to reply, then shrugged. 'I think we should agree to differ on that. Otherwise we'll spend all our time arguing!'

Emma nodded and turned towards the house. 'What did you do before you joined Mr Adams?'

'I was in the regular army—parachute regiment. I had a pretty bad fall and was given extended leave. Brett heard about it—we were at school together and never lost touch—and invited me here to recuperate. I liked it so much he persuaded me to resign my commission and work for him permanently. And I must say I've never regretted it.'

'It's not a very secure job, though.'

'Why do you say that?'

'Well . . . racing drivers are pretty poor risks!'

'That's something we never think about,' Bill said emphatically. 'It would be disastrous for our morale if we did. Brett's sensitive to moods and no one who works for him ever thinks in terms of death.'

'You must all have remarkable self-control then.'

'We do. Brett commands a hell of a lot of respect, and everything's geared to his needs.'

'What about Cindy's needs?' Emma couldn't help asking, forgetting her earlier decision not to invlove Bill in her problems with her employer. 'Or doesn't she count?'

'Of course she does. But she's only a child.'

'And in my book children come first! Why have them if you ignore them like Mr Adams does?'

'If you were right in what you say, *you* wouldn't be here now,' Bill said sharply. 'It's because he's concerned for Cindy that he keeps trying to get the right person to look after her.'

'He's the right person.'

'Oh, come on, how many men do you know who look after their children?'

'I didn't mean it literally. What I meant is that no governess, however good she is, can replace a parent. Cindy needs her father's love and——'

'She has it.'

'She doesn't think so. Quite the opposite, in fact. If I——' Emma stopped with a shake of her head. 'Look, I'm sorry to take it out on you. I should be saying all this to Mr Adams. It's wrong of me to cristicise him behind his back.'

'But safer,' came the dry response. 'He doesn't take kindly to criticism—especially from newcomers. My advice is to wait till you've been here a while longer. You might find you'll change your opinions.'

She said nothing and he chuckled.

'You've a very expressive face, Emma, but I'll forgive you! Truth to tell I'm delighted you're concerned about Cindy. But you're worrying for nothing.'

'I hope so.'

They reached the front door, and as she moved to go in, he stopped her.

'How about changing your mind and having dinner with me? he asked.

'Not tonight. I feel I should have it with Cindy—if she turns up, that is!'

'If she doesn't, let me know and I'll join you. I'm a pushover for nursery meals!'

Smiling, Emma went inside. She was already feeling more at home. Her chat with Bill had helped, even though he had disagreed with her criticisms. But she felt him to be a friend, and knew she might have need of one if she decided to beard the lion in his den. If? Emma sighed. There was no if about it. It was simply a question of when.

Promptly at seven-thirty she went to the playroom. As she had anticipated, there was no sign of her charge, and she paced the room nervously, knowing this was their first battle of wills. Should she go in search of the child or ignore her absence completely? She'd wait a few minutes and see what transpired.

Wandering over to the window, she looked out at the garden again, still marvelling that only yesterday she had woken up in a thatched cottage in a small Cotswold village. How different it was from the one she had seen with Bill earlier today, with its verandaed houses and flower-filled gardens, its white stucco church shaded by palms, and its main street a hubbub of donkeys and bikes.

A slight sound behind her made her stiffen. Then came the creak of a door. She was sure it was Cindy but forced herself not to turn round.

'Daddy always likes me to be nice to visitors,' a cool little voice declared, 'so I'll have supper with you tonight.'

'That's very kind of you,' Emma responded, straight-faced. 'I'm glad I don't have to eat alone. I always prefer talking to someone.'

'Marilyn—my last governess—said children bored her.'

'They don't bore me. That's why I enjoy looking after them.'

'That's what Diana said—she was here before Marilyn—but she didn't mean it. She only came 'cos she wanted to marry Daddy, and when he didn't take any notice of her she left.'

Emma was still cogitating how best to reply, when Cindy caught hold of her arm.

'Would you like to see my bedroom?'

'I'd love to.' Delighted by the child's friendliness, Emma went with her.

She had been into it only briefly before, and she let Cindy show her around. No expense had been spared to make it a little girl's dream. The walls were white and hand-painted with delicate flowers which matched those embroidered on the covered bedhead and duvet. The dressing table and bedside tables were in bleached mahogany, and the same wood fronted one entire wall, sections of which slid back to show row upon row of clothes.

'My daddy spoils me,' Cindy stated. 'He buys me everything I want.'

'You're a lucky girl.'

'Did your daddy spoil *you*?'

'I don't remember my father,' Emma replied. 'He died when I was two.'

Cindy stared at her for a moment. 'My mummy died when I was five,' she said finally, 'and I remember her all the time. But I love my daddy best. He's the nicest in the world.'

There the child went again! Setting her father up as an idol. Emma's anxiety deepened, but she pushed it aside and took one of the dresses off the rack.

'How pretty this is. I love pink.'

'Me too. It's my favourite colour. Mummy always wore it. Would you like to see her picture?'

Without waiting for an answer, Cindy ran over to her dressing table and from the top drawer took out a silver-framed photograph.

Even as Emma found herself wondering why the picture wasn't on display, she was caught by the beauty of the face staring up at her. Clear skin, silver-blonde hair and madonna-like features were set off by a cool smile that was echoed in the deep blue eyes.

'Your mother was very beautiful,' Emma said

softly. 'Why don't you keep the photograph on your dressing table, or by your bed?'

'Daddy doesn't want me to. He says it's mor—morbid.' Cindy returned it to the drawer. 'Do you think he's right?'

Emma hesitated, loath to make Cindy feel her father was wrong, yet unwilling to lie.

'It depends whether looking at the picture makes you happy or sad,' she prevaricated. 'If it makes you happy, then I don't see why you shouldn't keep it out. But if it makes you sad, then it's probably better to do as your father says.'

Cindy pondered this, than snatched the dress Emma was still holding and stuffed it back into her wardrobe.

'Let's play Monopoly.'

'We'll be having supper any minute.'

'I don't care. Supper can wait.'

Mutinously Cindy rushed back to the playroom and brought out the game from one of the cupboards. She set it up on a table by the window, and seated herself in front of it.

'Come on,' she ordered. 'I'm ready.'

'So am I—but for supper.' Emma decided that humour, rather than authority, might win the day with her stubborn little charge. 'If I don't eat soon I'll fall down.'

'Why?'

'Because I've got hollow legs and have to fill them with food!'

Cindy shrieked with laughter and fell on the floor in simulation of what Emma had said.

Walking in on this scene of mirth, Maria grinned as she set several silver-covered dishes on the hotplate in the centre of the table. A delicious smell wafted into the room as she lifted the lids to reveal a juicy pile of lamb chops, steaming rice jewelled with diced red, green and yellow peppers, and a mound of fried aubergine.

'I thought you said we weren't going to have a proper dinner at night,' Cindy commented.

'We're not—starting from tomorrow. But I didn't know how much you'd had for lunch.'

'I only had a potato. I was waiting for you, but you came late.'

Emma was touched by the poignancy of this remark, and distressed to think the child had barely eaten all day and no one had seemed to know or care.

'Daddy wanted me to have lunch with him, but I told him I was too busy,' Cindy went on, eagerly tackling her food.

Emma was sure the child was parroting the excuse her father usually gave to her, and her temper rose. The damned man wouldn't even know if Cindy starved all day! Nor did he seem to realise how insecure she was.

Remembering her conversation with Bill, she fought back her anger, knowing she had to bide her time. To rush in and accuse her employer of being unloving to his daughter would only result in her own dismissal and do Cindy no good whatsoever. She must marshal her facts and present him with an irrefutable assessment of the child's emotional state. Only then would she have a chance of arousing his conscience and get him to act the father proper.

But what if he refused? It was a question she dared not answer.

CHAPTER THREE

NEXT morning Cindy's lessons with Emma began. She was very bright, and after a battle of wills that lasted a couple of days, she became an attentive pupil as long as her interest was held. The moment it wandered, so did Cindy!

But Emma soon learned how to handle her. Realising the child could be cajoled and not ordered, she always started the day with the subject Cindy liked least—arithmetic—and ended it with the one she liked best, English. She was particularly good at creative writing, and let her imagination run as wild as it did in real life!

'How long are you going to stay with me?' Cindy asked one morning as she struggled with her hated sums.

'Until you go to boarding-school.'

'I'm lucky to be going away to school, aren't I?'

Emma paused. 'Are you looking forward to it?' she countered.

An odd expression crossed Cindy's face. ''Course I am. Daddy wants me to go.'

'I know. But how do you feel about it?'

'I want to do what Daddy wants. Then he'll love me.'

'I'm sure he loves you anyway.'

'He loves me more when I do as he tells me.'

Emma bit back a sigh, seeing this comment as yet another sign of Cindy's insecurity. How she longed to get Brett Adams by the scruff of the neck and shake

36

some sense into him! Didn't he know that clothes and toys were no substitute for his time and affection?

It was a question she could no longer leave unanswered, and she made up her mind to tackle him when next they met. Bill had urged her to get to know her employer first, had even suggested she might change her mind when she did. Fat chance! If anything, her opinion of him had sunk lower this past week, for he had spent barely an hour with his daughter in seven days.

'I've finished my sums,' Cindy cried, rushing over with her exercise book. 'You want to see?'

Emma looked at the two pages of badly written figures. The work was full of careless mistakes—only four of the ten sums were correct—and she gently explained why the others were wrong. For someone so insecure, criticism had to be carefully tempered.

'Sums aren't your favourite subject, are they?' she chided.

'No. I like reading and writing best.'

'We can't always do the things we like.'

'Daddy does. He loves racing and won't do anything else.'

Chickening out of continuing this discussion, Emma closed the exercise book and stood up.

'I think we've done enough lessons for this morning. How about a swim before lunch? Then this afternoon you can do some sewing.'

Cindy gave a whoop of joy. She had proved surprisingly adept on the machine, sufficiently so for Emma to suggest she now make something more mind-stretching than a scarf! 'I'll make you a dress,' she said jauntily.

Emma was touched. 'That's sweet of you, darling, but I don't think you should be quite so ambitious. Besides, we haven't any material.'

'We can buy some in Embira.'

Emma hesitated. She didn't drive—even if there was a car available to her—and she was pretty sure her employer wouldn't want her taking Cindy on a bus, which in this part of the country was likely to be jam-packed with people and livestock.

'How do you usually get there?' she asked.

'Daddy takes me. And if he's too busy, he asks Bill.'

That was more like it, Emma thought cynically, for no way could she see her employer wandering round the shops with his daughter.

'I think we can manage for the moment,' she said. 'I've just remembered, I brought some red cotton with me from England and you can make an apron for Maria.'

The afternoon couldn't have gone better. Cindy cut and sewed happily, and when Maria brought in her supper, she triumphantly handed her the finished garment.

"Muito obrigado," the maid cried her thanks. 'You is clever girl!'

'Show it to Daddy when you see him,' came the instant response.

Nodding, Maria left them, and Cindy tackled her meal with the hunger of the just, then, tired from sewing, offered none of her usual arguments about not going to bed. Only as she reached the threshold of the nursery did she pause.

'Will you say good night to me, Emma?'

'Don't I always?' Emma smiled. 'Good night darling.'

'I meant for you to come to my room and say it.'

Hiding her pleasure, Emma nodded. It was the first sign of warmth Cindy had shown her. Poor kid. She had so little affection in her life.

She was still musing over this when she went into Cindy's room. She was already in bed, and with her

hair loosened and faintly wavy now it was free of its
confining plaits, she barely looked the seven-year-old
she was. Her pink nightdress gave a bloom to her
pale skin, and Emma suddenly envisaged her as she
would be ten years from now: bright-eyed, intelligent
and extremely pretty. But, then, why shouldn't she
be, with a stunningly beautiful mother and a father
with enough insolent sex appeal to turn the head of
the Sphinx!

Emma perched on the bed. 'That's a pretty
nightdress.'

'Daddy went specially to Rio to buy it for me. He
chooses all my clothes.'

Emma swallowed hard. Maria had told her only
yesterday that they all came from a shop in Embira,
the proprietor picking them personally and delivering
them to the house.

'Sometimes Cindy no like, but mos' often she keep
all. The boss he generous father.'

In material things only, Emma thought now, and
swept the little girl up into a rollicking hug.

'Would you like me to read you a story?' she
asked.

Soon they were both immersed in *Alice in
Wonderland*, Emma so engrossed that it was some
while before she realised Cindy had fallen asleep.
Shutting the book, she stared at the perky little face.
Tenderness tugged at her heart, and she vowed to
speak to Brett Adams this very evening.

The prospect was sufficiently daunting to rob her of
appetite, and she did little more than push her dinner
around her plate, earning Maria's disapproval when
she came to collect her tray.

'Is Mr Adams in?' she asked the maid.

'He jus' finish eating.'

Emma decided to see him at once. The longer she
put it off, the more nervous she'd get. But first she'd

change into something more befitting a governess than the denim skirt and top she normally wore!

Some fifteen minutes later, in a demure shirtdress the same toffee-gold colour as her hair, which she'd carefully smoothed into a page-boy bob, she went downstairs.

Laughter and voices came from the lounge, and she assumed her employer was having an after-dinner drink with his team: an engineer, four mechanics and two Brazilian boys whose sole duty it was to nurse the cars night and day! She knew all of them by sight, for they ate in the house, though they lived in a guest bungalow on the far side of the swimming pool.

Emma knocked on the door, but the laughter was so loud no one heard so, drawing a deep breath, she turned the handle and went in.

All sound stopped, and eyes of varying colour stared at her. Emma stood where she was, shaking inside but giving no sign of it in her erect carriage and cool expression. A swift glance at the lounging figures told her Brett Adams was not among them.

'Sorry to barge in,' she apologised. 'I'm looking for——'

'Don't be sorry,' Bill cut in, rising and coming towards her. 'Everyone's been dying to meet you since you arrived.'

Drawing her forward, he made the introductions. The team were all British, apart from the two Brazilians, and in their late twenties to mid-thirties, with the easy-going manners of men used to being in the public eye. They each vied for her attention, plying her with drinks, which she refused, and with coffee, which she accepted.

'You must have a special hide-out,' Martin Dolomore, the engineer teased. 'I've wandered round in the evening looking for you but could never find you.'

'Maybe you don't use the right aftershave!' someone piped in.

'I generally go to bed early,' Emma smiled. 'Cindy wakes with the lark.'

'Too many early nights are bad for you,' Martin assured her. 'Makes the liver sluggish! What you need is some exercise, and I can personally recommend the discothèque in Embira. Fancy trying it tonight?'

'May I take a rain check?' Emma smiled, thinking it wiser not to get involved with any of these men.

'Only if you promise to say yes to me another night.'

'She'd be crazy to say yes to you any night!' Bill quipped.

There was a burst of good-natured laughter, in which Emma joined, the sound dying in her throat as her employer sauntered in through the French windows. In tight-fitting black slacks and white silk sweater he was as informally dressed as everyone else, yet whereas they looked relaxed, even faintly dishevelled, he exuded an aura of sensual elegance.

'What's the joke, boys?' he asked. 'Are you——' At the sight of Emma his good humour vanished. 'Good evening, Miss Fielding,' he said coldly. 'Where's Cindy?'

'Asleep. It's nine o'clock.'

He moved over to the drinks tray and poured himself a whisky and soda. 'So you felt in need of entertainment?' he commented, swinging round and giving her another cold stare.

'She's pretty hard to entertain,' Martin chuckled. 'We had to forcibly stop her running away.'

'Really?'

The scepticism was obvious, and Emma flushed

with anger. Did he think she had come down here to find herself a man?

'I was looking for you, Mr Adams,' she said. 'I'd like to talk to you.'

'It's that fatal charm of yours, Brett,' a young mechanic with tow-coloured hair chortled.

Ignoring him, Brett Adams nodded for Emma to follow him, and went into an office cum study on the other side of the hall. It was furnished with a teak desk and black leather armchairs, and he perched on the edge of the desk and signalled her to take a seat.

'Well, Miss Fielding?'

Emma's courage ebbed. What was there about this man that she found so daunting?

'I—er—I want to talk to you about C-Cindy. I thought you'd like to know how we were getting on.'

'Only if you have any problems with her. Otherwise I'm content to leave her to you.'

'That's obvious!'

The words burst out of their own volition, and sherry-brown eyes narrowed on her.

'What exactly does that mean, Miss Fielding? I've no time for games.'

'Nor have I. I'm deadly serious.'

'About what?'

'Cindy. She's extremely unhappy.'

'That's why I employed you—to make her happy.'

'I'm her governess, not a surrogate parent!'

There was a deathly hush. The lean jawline tightened and the long leg that had been swinging idly back and forth, stilled.

'I beg your pardon?'

'It isn't my pardon you should beg, Mr Adams, it's your daughter's! If you were a proper father and not a remote hero on a racing track, she'd be a——'

'How dare you talk to me like that?' he cut in furiously, his eyes glittering with red sparks.

'I dare for Cindy's sake,' Emma cried. 'She's desperately miserable and I'm afraid for her sanity.'

'Her sanity?' The man's expression went from anger to astonishment. 'Aren't you dramatising the situation?'

'No, I'm not. It happens to be the truth.'

'Well, you've attracted my attention, Miss Fielding, and since that's obviously what you intended . . .'

The raising of a finely arched eyebrow said far more, and Emma longed to hit him. Conceited swine!

'You think that's why I said it?' Her voice, normally liquid gold, turned acid. 'I don't know where you found all the previous governesses you employed, from the back pages of a porno magazine I should think, but I assure you the last thing I want is your attention. I'd rather bed down with a boa constrictor! And now we've got that out the way, let's get back to your daughter. She's convinced you don't love her and it's affecting her behaviour. If you were with her more often you'd see it for yourself.'

Angry red suffused the man's face, and despairingly Emma knew she had gone too far. He was right in saying she was overly dramatic, but it was the only way she knew of getting him to listen to her. How awful if she'd made him too furious to do so! That bit about the boa constrictor had been unduly strong. But he'd had no business comparing her with the other governesses he'd employed!

'I'm sorry I was rude,' she said stiffly. 'But you provoked me.'

'What do you think you did to me—calling my daughter insane?'

'I didn't! I said I fear for her sanity. The line between fantasy and reality is a very fine one, Mr Adams, and if children are miserable with the reality of a situation, they'll often retreat into make-believe.'

'What's the harm in that?'

Tilting his head, the man drained his drink. The light from a standard lamp caught his throat and Emma noticed how strong it was. Hadn't she read somewhere that racing drivers needed well-muscled necks because of the dangers of whiplash?

'When I was a youngster,' he went on, 'I was always imagining things. At one point I believed I was Long John Silver, and walked round with a limp for weeks!'

'If Cindy isn't given the love she needs,' Emma returned, 'she'll be an emotional cripple for life!'

With an angry thud, Brett Adams banged down his glass and stood up. Moving over to the window, he looked out, rubbing one long-fingered hand along the back of his neck, as if trying to relieve tension. It surprised Emma, for she had considered him a nerveless man.

'I appreciate you're a trained nursery school teacher,' he said, voice dry as long-stored tinder. 'But that hardly qualifies you to judge a child's mental state.'

'If you hear me out, I think you'll agree with my assessment.'

Leaning against the side of the frame, he faced her, arms folded across his chest. 'Very well, I'm listening.'

With the head or the heart? she wondered, but aloud said, 'From the moment I came here, Cindy's been telling me how close you are to her—even though I can see for myself that you aren't! She also says she goes all over the world with you, and watches all your races.'

'That's absolute rot! I've taken her on my travels a couple of times, but she's never seen me race. Never. In fact my staff have strict instructions not even to let her know when I'm on the track!'

'That's what I thought,' Emma sighed. 'All the

same, she believes everything she's told me. The other day she informed me she'd been in your car when you broke the world speed record! When I teased her for pretending, she cried for an hour, and even now she won't admit she was making it up. And there've been many similar incidents. If you don't believe me, ask Bill. He's heard quite a few of the things she's said.'

In silence the man averted his head. The lamps on the veranda threw his body into relief, making his shoulders look broader and his thick mane of hair darker. He raked his hand through it, his uplifted arm pulling his sweater tight, showing the ripple of muscle in the firm back.

'I find this terribly hard to take in,' he said heavily. 'Cindy has everything a child could want. Clothes, toys, people to take care of her and——'

'Everything except parents to love her!' Emma cut in brutally.

'Damn you!' The man spun round. 'Her mother's dead, Miss Fielding, and all the will in the world can't resurrect her!'

'But her father's alive!' Emma came back at him. 'And he should accept his responsibilities.'

'How dare you judge me when you don't know the situation?'

'I know enough to realise all you care about is winning your stupid races! You're nothing more than an overgrown schoolboy who should never have had a child!'

Brett Adams glared at her, his mouth moving soundlessly, his hands clenching and unclenching as if aching to twine themselves around her throat. Knowing that when next he spoke, it would be to tell her she was fired, Emma decided she might as well go out with all flags flying.

'It's time someone told you the truth, Mr Adams.

Cindy's sick with love for you, yet for all the notice you take of her, you might as well be as dead as your wife!'

'How dare you!' Lunging forward, he shook her furiously, then threw her away from him with such violence that she slipped and fell, slithering along the shiny floor like a discarded doll.

Instantly he was across the room and picking her up, his hands shaking, his face pale.

'God! I'm sorry—so sorry. I never lose my temper, but you—you . . .'

'It was my fault too,' she murmured as he half-carried her to a chair. 'I'd no right to say what I did.'

'You care about Cindy,' he muttered. 'That gives you the right. And I also owe you an explanation.'

He returned to sit at his desk and watching him, Emma knew that if she had any sense she'd walk out and not stop until she'd put the ocean between herself and this tormented man. But memory of the little girl upstairs kept her where she was.

'The only reason I keep away from Cindy,' he began, 'is because I love her and don't want to hurt her.'

'That doesn't make sense!'

'It does if you think about it. I'm in a dangerous profession, Miss Fielding, and I don't want her being dependent on me for her happiness.'

'You can't prevent it! You're her father and she loves and needs you. Don't you know that by keeping her at arm's length you're getting her to mourn for you as if you're already dead?'

The man slumped back in his chair, and Emma studied the lean face, the sensuous mouth now pulled tight, the mocking eyes dark with shadows, and wondered what tragic thoughts filled his mind. That he was in a hell of his own, was evident, and she wished she knew what had put him there.

'I've overstepped the mark again, Mr Adams, and I'm sorry. But no child—nobody, in fact—can be happy without love.'

'There speaks a romantic! But I'm a realist, and I regard love as a chain that ties you down.'

'It didn't stop you marrying!'

'What the hell business is that of yours?'

Emma sighed and stood up, knowing further discussion was impossible. 'When do you wish me to go?'

'Go where?'

'To leave. After the things I've said, you won't——'

'Stop trying to read my mind! If I wanted to fire you, I'd have done so the minute you started in on me. But as I've just said, you care about Cindy and that makes you the ideal person to look after her. Now if you'll excuse me, I've work to do.'

Though glad not to be dismissed, Emma saw problems in staying.

'It might be better if I left, Mr Adams.'

'For you and me, maybe, but not for my daughter. It would be wrong for you to leave her now she's fond of you.'

Emma was flabbergasted. 'I like the way you shelve your responsibility on to me!'

'I'm glad to hear it. Then you'll stay?'

'That wasn't what I meant!'

'I know. But the discussion's closed.' He put the tips of his fingers together. 'So what's it to be? Are you going or staying?'

'Staying,' she said bitterly. 'I'd never desert an orphan.'

'Cindy isn't . . .' Understanding hit him, and angry colour stained his high cheekbones. 'You pack a mean punch for a pint-sized blonde.'

'I'm surprised you feel it,' she said from the door, and banged it shut behind her.

Too overwrought by her conversation with Brett Adams to return to her room, Emma went for a walk.

It was a moon-bright night and the waters of the estuary glittered silver, the trees black against the star-studded sky. The heady scent of tobacco plants filtered the air, accompanied by the soft cry of a bird nesting in a tree. How peaceful it was, so different from the drama that had just ensued in the house.

She was still not certain she had done the right thing in agreeing to stay on. She was fond of Cindy, and would become increasingly so the longer she knew her, which could well lead to another confrontation with the child's father.

What a complicated man he was! She paused by the swimming pool to stare into the floodlit water. Tortuously analytical too, if the reasons he had given for remaining detached from his daughter were anything to go by.

'Emma?'

A man's voice called her name and she swung round, her slender body tensing. But it was Bill who stepped from the shadows, his neat-featured face anxious. How stupid of her to think it might have been her employer. She was always Miss Fielding to him.

'I wondered where you'd got to,' he said. 'I was worried.'

'Did you think I'd come here to drown myself?'

'Or the boss!'

'I would—if I thought it would achieve anything!'

'You mean all that shouting in the study came to nothing?'

'I'm afraid so.'

'I've never known him lose his temper like that,' Bill went on. 'We half-expected you to come to blows!'

She shrugged, unwilling to admit they nearly had. Her thigh still hurt where she had fallen on it.

'I said some pretty rough things to him about Cindy,' she confessed, moving away from the pool.

'What sort of things—or don't you want to talk about it?'

Emma hesitated, debating whether it was disloyal to tell Bill what had transpired. Yet since she'd told Brett Adams that Bill had noticed Cindy's behaviour too, it seemed only fair to be frank with him.

Briefly she recounted the gist of the conversation, and though Bill heard her out in silence, the slowing of his step showed she had given him considerable food for thought.

'You honestly think it would solve Cindy's problems if Brett spent more time with her?' he asked finally.

'There's no doubt of it. He doesn't disagree with me either. He simply says he won't act differently— for all the reasons I've given you.'

'They're valid ones, you know.'

'You think so? If he were killed, wouldn't it at least be better if Cindy had happy memories of her father?'

'Don't talk of his being killed,' Bill said quickly. 'In this game one should——'

'Racing isn't a game,' Emma exclaimed. 'It's a madness! And what's it all for anyway? It doesn't achieve anything.'

'On the contrary. Everything we learn on the track goes to make cars safer. You wouldn't call test-pilots childish, would you?'

'You can't compare the two. They don't do it for adulation or the money.'

'Neither do people like Brett. They do it for the challenge, because they love testing their skill and courage.'

'To say nothing of the fame it brings them, or the women!'

'Those things don't motivate Brett. He'd give up racing tomorrow if . . .'

Discretion curbed Bill's tongue, and Emma could have shaken him. She'd give anything to know what motivated her arrogant employer but, short of bearding him and asking him, was no nearer finding out.

'I'm glad you aren't leaving us,' Bill said suddenly. 'Having you here puts the sun in my day.'

It was such a change of conversation that Emma was momentarily at a loss how to reply.

'I could say a whole lot more,' he went on, 'but I don't want to embarrass you.' He kicked at a stone in his path. 'I guess you know what I'm trying to say, anyway.'

She debated whether to play the innocent, then decided on truthfulness. 'I think so.'

'And?'

'We hardly know each other.

'That's easily remedied! Just say the word.'

She looked away. 'It would have to be no, I'm afraid.'

'I see.' His voice was flat, and they walked for several minutes before he spoke again. 'I should have taken notice of my horoscope this morning,' he murmured finally. 'It said: Don't try your luck!'

Emma laughed, relieved he could joke about it. 'I'm not your type anyway—a serious-minded nursery school teacher who loathes motor racing!'

'We can still be friends, though?' he questioned.

'Certainly.'

'Then come out with me tonight.'

'It would be better psychology if you went with someone else.'

'To hell with psychology! Haven't you heard of the hair of the dog?'

She grinned, and sensing she was about to give in, Bill coaxed, 'Come on, Emma. Say yes.'

'I'd like to, but . . . well, I don't want to annoy Mr Adams any more than I've already done. And I've a feeling he wouldn't like me fraternising with any of his team.

'Fraternising?' Bill's pale blue eyes crinkled with amusement. 'We aren't enemy soldiers!'

'I know, but when I think how the other governesses behaved . . .'

'You're completely different. If the boss can't see it for himself, he's blind.'

'There are many things he can't see,' she rejoined.

'But good little girls are very noticeable,' Bill joked.

'You want to go out with a good girl?'

'Sure. There's a first time for everything!'

Laughing, she gave him a push, and he grabbed her hand and raced her back to the house.

'Get a jacket and we'll go into Embira,' he said. 'See you at the car in five minutes.'

Searching out a cardigan, Emma caught sight of herself in the mirror. How prim she looked in her shirtdress! But then she'd dressed for a meeting with her employer, not a date with Bill, whose easy charm could turn any girl's heart. Yet not her own, she knew, and wondered if she were covered by an invisible, bulletproof jacket that made her immune from Cupid's dart.

Chiding herself for being fanciful, she hurriedly changed into a candy-striped skirt and matching top, loose and easy, yet artfully cut to reveal what it pretended to conceal.

Driving into town in a highly tuned two-seater, she was glad she had agreed to go out. Staying in her

room night after night brooding over Cindy wouldn't
solve anything. She had to tackle the problem by
stealth: inveigle the child into her father's company
and make it impossible for him to ignore her.

'What do you fancy doing?' Bill broke into her
thoughts. 'We can go to the disco or have a drink
somewhere and talk.'

'A drink sounds fine—especially if it comes with a
triple-decker sandwich! I was so nervous of talking to
Mr Adams I barely ate any dinner.'

'Say no more, lady. I know where they do
marvellous snacks.'

His foot pressed hard on the accelerator and they
shot forward. Emma clutched at her seat, trying not
to notice how fast the tall palms were whizzing past.
It was only when they rounded a bend on what she
would have sworn was one wheel, that she begged
him to slow down.

'I'm only doing sixty,' he assured her, easing his
foot from the pedal.

'That's twenty miles an hour too fast for me!'

'Sorry.'

Obligingly he eased down further, and some quarter
of an hour later they reached Embira, a seaside town
with graceful old houses in the Portuguese style, and
modern hotels in the American.

'Somewhere they do marvellous snacks' turned out
to be a charming, wide-windowed restaurant on the
beach-front, with piped music wafting to them from
some hidden source as they stepped into a romantically
dim room decorated with huge shells and glittering
fishing nets. All around them casually garbed people
sat at tables, eating and drinking, while a milling
crowd half-hid the bar that ran along the nearside
wall.

'Brett's here,' Bill muttered. 'Sorry about that.'

'Don't be. I'm not his prisoner!'

A quick glance showed him perched on a bamboo stool by the bar, a girl either side of him.

'Pit followers,' Bill explained.

'What's that mean?' Emma was careful not to look in her employer's direction.

'When a car needs attention during a race, it draws into its own pit—or enclosure,' Bill explained. 'Hence the term.'

'Not a very pretty one.'

'Nor are the girls. Good lookers on the surface, but inside empty as used cartridges. Brett's the star attraction, of course, but if they can't have him they'll settle for any other member of the team.'

'How awful.'

'You don't think so when you're young!'

'Yes, junior!'

He squeezed her arm. 'Bite on a shrimp instead of me!'

'I'd love to!'

Hardly had they settled themselves at a table, when Brett Adams left the bar and did the same. He was the centre of a dozen men and women, and Emma recognised Martin, the engineer, and two other mechanics; the rest appeared to be Brazilians. Two tables were pushed together, and there was much laughter and talking before they began to study the menu.

The main attraction was the great man himself. Skin flushed, eyes gleaming, he was smiling at everyone. Was he drunk, Emma wondered, or buoyant with sexual excitement?

As she watched, a bottle-dyed redhead inched her chair closer to his and pressed herself against his side. He pulled away and she giggled and proceeded to curve her arm round his neck. He pushed her away again and turned his back on her, giving his attention to the brunette on the other side of him.

'Are these girls the local talent?' Emma enquired.

'Half of them. The rest follow us from country to country.'

'Can they afford it?'

'The men can!'

Did that include her employer? Emma longed to know, but resolutely held her tongue. He was now ignoring the brunette too, and chatting up a blonde opposite him as he sipped at a large whisky.

'Does Mr Adams drink when he's in training?' she couldn't help asking.

'He's pretty abstemious even when he isn't. That lethal-looking concoction in his hand is grape juice!'

A large shrimp salad was placed before Emma, and she stared at it, dismayed. The hunger she'd professed a short while ago had vanished the instant she'd walked into the restaurant and seen Brett. But she didn't want Bill to know, and made a valiant effort to eat. Luckily, once she started, her appetite returned and it wasn't long before every shrimp was gone.

'Sure you've had enough?' Bill teased as she delicately licked one finger.

'Quite sure! I feel a new woman.'

'With new ideas?'

'Only the old ones, I'm afraid.' Her expression grew serious. 'I mean it, Bill.'

'I know. And I'll stop teasing.' He eyed her glass. 'More wine?'

'No, thanks. But I'd love some coffee.'

'I'll go fetch it. It'll be quicker.' He rose and disappeared in the direction of the bar.

Reluctant to be seen by Brett, Emma slightly turned in her chair and kept her eyes on the table. A headache was threatening—not surprising considering the tension of this evening—and she longed for the quiet of her room.

'Bill deserted you?' an abrupt voice questioned,

and she was forced to turn and face the one man she didn't want to see.

'No, Mr Adams. He's gone to get me a coffee.'

'Tell him we're all going on to Toni's, will you? You're both welcome to join us.'

'I'll give him the message. But I'm going home.'

'Still angry with me, Miss Fielding?' The mocking smile on the lean face told her she was being baited. 'Why not forget our earlier contretemps? I have.'

'That doesn't endear you to me!'

'Pity.' Hands in the pockets of his trousers, the tightly stretched material drawing attention to his thickly muscled thighs, he rocked slightly back and forth. 'I don't want my daughter looked after by a porno model, as you so delicately put it, but I don't want a repressed spinster either! God knows what sort of adult she'd become.'

'Since you don't envisage being alive to see it, why worry?' Emma snapped.

Sherry-brown eyes blazed into hers. 'One day you'll go too far!'

'I'm happy to go now, Mr Adams. I'm sure you can find a replacement.'

'Without a doubt. But I'm not letting you cop out that easily. You'll stay till you take Cindy to school in England.'

'Will you want me to visit her there too? Even have her for the holiday, perhaps? Then you can cop out entirely.'

'Don't put ideas in my head!' He stepped back from her. 'Give Bill my message. And if I don't see you at Toni's, sweet dreams!'

She did not watch him return to his table, but guessed from the squeals of girlish delight, that he was once more being besieged.

A moment later Bill came back. 'Sorry I was so long but I couldn't get near the bar.'

He set down her coffee and she sipped it gratefully, surprised to see her hand shaking. That damned man!

'Mr Adams asked us to join him at Toni's,' she said.

'Great. You'll like it there. They've a fantastic pianist. Good as Brubeck.'

'Would you mind if I left it for another night? I've a rotten headache. If you could get me a taxi I'll——'

'Don't be daft! We can go to Toni's another time. Drink up and I'll take you home.'

On the way, he said casually, 'Your headache wouldn't have anything to do with the boss, would it? I know you and he don't see eye to eye over Cindy, but I'm sure he'll take note of what you said.'

Emma didn't agree, but held her tongue. Bill was trying to be fair, but it was as well to remember he was Brett Adams's friend as well as employee.

'The two of you are very different,' she murmured. 'How come you've remained friends?'

'Attraction of opposites, I suppose. Brett's easy to get on with, contrary to what you think, and once he gives his friendship, it's yours for life.'

'Even if you let him down?'

'Even then. He's the sort who'll always find excuses for you.'

'I can't imagine that,' she said bluntly. 'He strikes me as the unforgiving type.'

'It's his own mistakes he can't condone! But he's the exact opposite with everyone else. And where women are concerned, he's a pushover. I thought marrying Eileen would have taught him some sense, but it——' Bill broke off, looking distinctly uncomfortable. 'Sorry. I've no right to discuss Brett. He'd be furious if he knew.'

'You're not idly gossiping,' Emma consoled. 'He's Cindy's father and it would help if I understood him.'

'Not many people do.' Bill flashed his headlamps

and overtook a passing car that was doing a steady fifteen mph. 'Idiot driver,' he muttered, then lapsed into silence, showing the time for confidences had passed.

Emma sighed. Although curious to learn more about the man she worked for, it was probably safer if she didn't. You could more easily forget someone if you didn't know what made them tick.

The car drew to a stop outside the house and she got out. 'It was a lovely evening, Bill. I'm sorry I had to end it so early.'

'Does that mean we can have a repeat?'

'Any time!'

He came round the side of the car and kissed her cheek. 'I won't offer to see you to your room in case you think I've improper notions!'

'Haven't you?'

'Mind if I take the Fifth Amendment?'

Smiling, she went to her room. Her headache was worse and she took a couple of aspirins and slipped into her nightdress, a wisp of hyacinth blue with matching satin ribbons criss-crossing under the bust. It had been an extravagant going-away present from Dr Walpole and his wife, and Emma had thought it highly suitable to the glamorous six-month job she was going to.

Glamorous on the surface maybe, she thought wryly, but below seethed the problems and complexities of the most macho man she had met. But five months from now those problems would no longer be hers and bearing this firmly in mind she snuggled down to sleep.

CHAPTER FOUR

EMMA sat up in bed with a violent start, heart racing. Something had disturbed her. Remaining upright, she listened. Then she heard it again, a plaintive cry, eerie in the dark, silent night.

Slipping on her dressing-gown, she hurried along the corridor to Cindy's room. As she reached it, the cry came more clearly. Cindy must be having a nightmare. Softly Emma opened the door.

The little girl was curled up in a ball in bed, and Emma switched on the bedside lamp. Even in the dimness the child looked flushed, and she put her arm around the thin shoulder, dismayed to find it hot to the touch.

'What's the matter, darling?'

'I feel sick.'

'You've probably caught a chill. I'll take your temperature.'

She did, concerned to see it was very high. She nibbled on her lip, uncertain what to do. If Brett Adams were away, this would be solely her problem, but since he was here, she didn't see why he shouldn't take the responsibility. In fact it would darn well do him good!

On the other hand, children often ran high temperatures which only lasted a few hours, and she would look a real idiot if she panicked and called him unnecesarily. She would wait to see what happened. Anyway, bearing in mind the company he'd been

58

keeping earlier this evening, she doubted he'd be home yet!

'I'll give you a pill,' she said gently, 'and then a cool bed bath. It will help you feel better.'

Keeping up a cheerful flow of chatter, Emma sponged Cindy down, then helped her into a fresh nightdress.

'Would you like me to sit with you for a while?' she asked.

'I want you to stay all night.' A small hand reached out to clasp hers. 'I feel better when you're here.'

'Then I won't leave you. I'll push an armchair up to the bed and you can hold my hand again.'

Over-bright eyes watched anxiously as Emma settled herself, and only when Cindy could clasp her fingers, did the child relax and fall asleep.

Half an hour passed and Emma's arm grew numb. Carefully she tried to withdraw her hand, but Cindy woke up crying.

'Darling, don't,' Emma soothed. 'I'm still here. I haven't left you.'

'What's going on?' a deep voice enquired, and Emma turned to see her employer at the door, his suede jacket over his arm.

'Cindy has a temperature, and isn't feeling well.'

'She's prone to chills.' He came to the foot of the bed. 'There's no need to cry, Cindy. You're a big girl, not a baby.'

'I'm not a big girl.' The tears fell faster and her father frowned.

Emma looked at him beseechingly. But instead of moving closer to his daughter, he backed away.

'There's no need for you to stay up with her, Miss Fielding,' he said tersely. 'Call Maria. She's been with Cindy for years and knows how to manage her.'

'I don't want Maria,' Cindy wailed. 'I want Emma.'

'You can't expect her to stay up all night with you.'

'I don't mind,' Emma said swiftly.

'Please youself then.' He went to the door. 'Good night, Cindy. I'm sure you'll be OK in the morning.'

'Don't go, Daddy!'

'I must. I've a busy day tomorrow and need my sleep.'

He went out and the little girl burst into sobs. Emma rocked her back and forth, stroking her damp head and longing to hit her employer. What a heartless swine he was! How could any parent remain so detached when their child was ill?

'Daddy doesn't love me,' Cindy cried through her tears. 'He hates me 'cos Mummy ran away and it was all my fault.'

Shocked by the statement—it was one more puzzle for her to resolve—Emma none the less knew it was imperative for Cindy's peace of mind that she refute it.

'That's a silly thing for you to say, darling. Your mother was—was ill and died. That's quite different from going away and leaving you.'

'Mummy wasn't ill,' Cindy sobbed. 'She ran away 'cos I was naughty and she got killed. Miss Upton said so.'

'Who's Miss Upton?'

'She used to be my governess.'

'Then Miss Upton was a very silly lady who wasn't telling you the truth,' Emma stated firmly. 'If Daddy knew what she'd said, he'd be furious with her. He loves you more than anyone else in the world. Why else do you think he asked me to come all the way from England to look after you?'

Cindy leaned back in Emma's arms and searched her face. 'Did he tell you he loves me?'

'He most definitely did,' Emma lied, and was rewarded by a bright smile.

Even so, it was some time before Cindy fell asleep

and Emma could settle her back on her pillows and resume her seat by the bed. She managed to doze fitfully for what was left of the night, but had a cracking headache when Maria crept in at six-thirty.

'Mr Adams say you go sleep,' she whispered. 'I stay here.'

Gratefully Emma returned to her room, and did not surface again till eleven, when she had a quick shower, donned a cotton dress and went to see her charge.

She pondered on what Cindy had said about her mother. Even if the woman had really walked out on her husband, what evil motive had made Miss Upton put the blame on the child? The only explanation was that Cindy had tried her patience and the governess had wanted to hurt her. Yet it was a monstrous thing to have said, particularly as Brett Adams's unloving attitude had made his daughter see his behaviour as retribution.

Emma was half-way along the corridor when a woebegone Maria came out of the playroom.

'Doctor an' Mr Adams with Cindy,' she announced. 'Her fever bad.'

How frightening the word fever sounded. Heart thumping, Emma hovered in the corridor, and moments later saw her employer and a stocky, middle aged Brazilian emerge from the night nursery.

Over the man's shoulder, Brett Adams beckoned her. 'I didn't realise you were awake. I hope you managed to get some sleep?'

'Enough.' She wondered how well his conscience had let him rest. 'How's Cindy?' she questioned the doctor.

'It's a chill,' he replied. 'I'll call in again tomorrow unless I hear from you.'

Only when he had gone, did Emma look her employer directly in the face.

'May I speak to you privately?'

'What's it this time?' Hands on the hips of his tight white jeans, he looked down his patrician nose at her. 'I thought we'd said all there was to say last night.'

'Not quite.'

With a resigned shrug he led the way into the playroom, every inch of his tall frame indicating impatience.

'Well, out with it.'

Emma straightened her shoulders. Since he had no intention of making it easy for her, she saw no reason to be diplomatic.

'Last night Cindy told me Miss Upton said you blamed your daughter for your wife leaving you and subsequently dying.'

'*What?*' Muscles bunched in the man's throat.

'That's why Cindy thinks you don't love her, and won't spend any time with her.'

With a muffled oath he turned away, and Emma regarded him with a faint stirring of sympathy.

'I'm sorry I had to mention it, Mr Adams, but it's a dreadful burden for a child—for anyone—to carry.'

'I agree. I'll talk to her about it as soon as she's well. Meanwhile . . .' He swung round on Emma, his eyes hooded. 'Meanwhile I'd be obliged if you stopped prying into my affairs. I engaged you as a governess, not an inquisitor!'

This was such an unjust accusation that Emma couldn't let it go unremarked.

'If you think I forced Cindy's confidence you can think again! I don't give a damn what you do with your life, except where it affects your daughter!'

Muttering beneath his breath, he strode to the door.

'That's right,' she called, 'run away! That's your answer to everything where your child's concerned.

You may be a genius in a car, but you're a wash-out as a father!'

He stopped in his tracks, and if looks could have killed, Emma knew she would have been taken from the room feet first.

'I've told you why I stay away from her,' he grated. 'Why can't you leave well alone!'

'Because things aren't well! Talk to any psychologist about the way you're treating Cindy. And if they go along with it, I'll go down on my knees and lick your boots!'

She glared at him defiantly, her slender body tense, her small breasts rising and falling. Their eyes met, and his dropped first.

'Are you trying to reform me?' he asked tonelessly.

'No, Mr Adams. Your life is yours to throw away, if that's what you want. But I can't stand by and watch you destroy your child's!'

'You mean you'll leave if I don't do as you ask?'

'No. I promised I'd stay till Cindy goes to school and I won't go back on my word.'

'Good. Then you've nothing to blackmail me with!'

Before she could retort, he was gone.

Cindy's chill proved to be far more than that, for in the early evening her temperature soared and she developed a bronchial cough.

'She may be sickening for something,' Dr da Silva said when he returned to re-examine her. 'She'll bear watching.'

Emma decided to sleep in the child's room, and had her bed moved in. Cindy perked up at this, but soon grew listless again. She fell asleep quite quickly, and Emma was able to leave Maria with her while she went for her nightly stroll in the garden.

She was too restless to remain outside for long, and she returned to the house. She heard laughter and voices coming from the main reception room,

and though it was hard to make out any individual
one, she wouldn't have been surprised if her
employer's was among them. He hadn't been near his
daughter all day, though she had heard him speaking
to the doctor when he had called back that evening.

Sighing, she mounted the stairs, and was half-way
up when she heard a choking cry. Taking the rest of
the flight at a run, she tore into the bedroom, where
a frightened Maria had her arms round the wheezing
child.

'Ask Mr Adams to call the doctor,' Emma ordered
softly, and as the maid scurried out she propped
Cindy up with pillows and murmured to her
reassuringly.

'My chest hurts,' the little girl croaked.

'I know, darling. That's why it's better if you don't
talk.'

'Maria says Cindy has trouble breathing,' Brett
Adams said from the door.

At sight of him Cindy stretched out her arms, the
exertion bringing on another coughing spasm. 'Hold
me, Daddy,' she gasped.

Swiftly he was beside her and lifting her into his
arms. 'No talking, little one,' he ordered. 'It will
make your cough worse.'

Cindy nestled close, and he looked down at her.
His clenched jaw indicated tension, though his lowered
lids made his expression unreadable, so Emma could
not tell if he was suffering pangs of guilt or genuine
fear for his daughter's well-being.

By the time the doctor arrived, Cindy had drifted
off to sleep and barely stirred as she was examined.

'I'm not sure what's wrong with her,' he declared,
'but I'd feel happier if she was in hospital.'

'Hospital?' A nerve twitched in Brett Adams's lean
cheek. 'Can't we bring a nurse here?'

'Of course. But in hospital everything's to hand. I really think it would be advisable.'

'I don't want her to go to Embira,' Brett Adams stated. 'A friend of mine runs a clinic in Rio and I'll take her there.'

'You've missed the last plane,' Dr da Silva said, 'and quite honestly, I'd like her hospitalised as soon as possible.'

'I'll hire a private plane, then.' The answer was incisive and brooked no argument. 'If you could arrange for a nurse and anything else that may be necessary . . .' He glanced at Emma. 'Get Cindy ready, will you? I'll be up for her as soon as I've made the arrangements. And you'd better come too. Once she's on the mend, she'll need entertaining.'

Let that day only come, Emma prayed, as two hours later she sat beside a nurse in the executive jet bearing them north through the clear night sky. For once she felt no fear of flying, all her concern centred on the child lying limp in her father's arms.

The change in him astounded her. Was it caused by guilty conscience or the realisation that he had needlessly hurt both himself and Cindy by shutting her out of his life? What a pity it had taken an emergency to get him to show his feelings. And how tragic if his new attitude had come too late!

She must have dozed, for the changing sound of the aircraft's engines alerted her to their descent. Beside her, the nurse was fast asleep, but Brett Adams didn't appear to have moved since boarding the plane. He was still holding Cindy, and Emma was sure he had had no sleep. Yet he showed no fatigue, his mouth firm as always, his eyes clear and sharp.

The plane dropped lower and instinctively Emma clutched at her arm rests. Wheels screeched on the tarmac, a bolted-down vase rattled, then stilled as the aircraft came to a halt.

The nurse, jolted awake, moved across to wrap Cindy up more warmly, but when she went to take hold of her, the man shook his head.

'Where are we, Daddy?' Cindy cried thickly.

'In Rio, angel. I'm taking you to a clinic where they'll make you better.'

Holding her carefully, he went down the aircraft steps to where an ambulance awaited them.

'I've arranged for a car and chauffeur to take you straight to the hotel,' he told Emma over his shoulder.

'I'd rather go with you to the clinic.'

With a nod, he climbed into the ambulance with the nurse, leaving Emma to walk across to the car. His foresight had surprised her, though it shouldn't have. After all, he was used to keeping his head in tricky situations, an ability that had taken him to the top of his profession. Feelings of consideration had nothing to do with his ordering her a car.

Yet was this true? Yesterday she would have had no doubts, but tonight, recalling the hours he had nursed Cindy, she realised how much of an enigma he was. Indeed the more she saw of him, the less she understood him.

Emma had forgotten to ask Brett Adams the address of the clinic, so in the best Hollywood tradition she told her driver to 'Follow that white car'.

It was an order she regretted every second of the next fifteen minutes as their limousine hurtled through the packed streets of Rio, inches behind the ambulance.

Cars seem to come at them from all directions, traffic lights were regarded as an insult as drivers, forced to stop at red, revved menacingly till they saw green, then moved forward at such speed that any hapless pedestrian half-way across the road, considered himself lucky to reach the other side.

Agitated by the events of the past twenty-four hours, Emma clutched at her seat and fatalistically decided that what would be would be. She was agreeably surprised, therefore, when the sudden silence told her they had arrived at their destination, a modern, white stone building of five storeys in a wide, tree-lined avenue.

Entering the air-conditioned lobby, she was in time to see lift doors close behind her employer's tall frame, and she headed for the reception desk.

Moments later she was shown to a waiting-room on the ground floor, in which she paced anxiously before finally sitting down and attempting to relax.

The magazines on the centre table were all in Portuguese, and the English one she eventually found was a scientific journal that could have been written in Esperanto for all she could make of it.

Resolutely she shut her eyes, and was in a state of suspension between daydreaming and sleep, when she felt she was being watched. Lifting her lids, she saw her employer staring down at her.

She went to speak, but he forestalled her. 'No news yet. Cindy's having tests and we won't know results till later. So we may as well leave.'

'Don't you think I should stay with her?' Emma asked. 'She must be nervous on her own.'

'She's too heavily sedated to know anything.'

But as Emma followed him out to the car, she was determined to return to the clinic as soon as she'd unpacked. Sleepy or not, she felt Cindy would want a familiar face with her.

Their journey to the hotel was a sedate one. The chauffeur—infinitely conscious of his famous passenger—drove with the utmost care, yet Emma could not relax. She was too conscious of the man beside her, too aware of his maleness and vibrant energy. From the corner of her eye she watched him, his hands idle on his lap, beautiful narrow hands with long supple fingers and strong wrists, as she knew they had to be to control a car at the death-dicing speeds at which he drove.

'You must be tired,' he said unexpectedly. 'You were on tenterhooks on the plane.'

'How could you tell?'

'You didn't once look out of the window, and acted like a startled rabbit every time there was the slightest tremor in the cabin!'

'We all have our phobias,' she said shortly.

'True. My particular one is being driven. If there's anyone else but me behind the wheel, I pretend I'm not in the car.'

Emma wasn't sure if he was being serious or teasing, and was still wondering about it when they reached their hotel, a huge skyscraper standing on the fabulous curving bay that made up Copacabana beach.

After all she had heard about this famous beach, her first sight of it was incredibly disappointing. True, there was a vast expanse of blue-grey water with a magnificent stretch of powder-white sand, and a wonderful wide esplanade along which people were strolling. But cars streamed non-stop along the road, and the singular absence of greenery and trees, together with the vast edifices of countless hotels stretching around the bay, turned the entire scene into the epitome of a concrete jungle.

But once inside the hotel she was overwhelmed by the lofty foyer with its glittering crystal lights and marble floor, vast reception desk and innumerable pageboys waiting to do your bidding.

Watching Brett sign in, she couldn't help noticing he was the cynosure of all eyes—people nudging each other and pointing him out. Yet even if he weren't a famous personality, his bearing and brooding magnetism would have drawn the eye of any woman, and she wondered for the first time whether his wife had left him because he had been unfaithful to her.

Thinking of the pit followers, it seemed a possibility. But if that were the case, why hadn't Mrs Adams taken Cindy with her? There were many questions she would have liked answered, but as her employer was her only source, she would have to batten down her curiosity. Unless she could get him to talk about it—as unlikely as a boa constrictor giving you a gentle hug!

She heard her name being called, and saw Brett waiting at one of the lifts. Quickly she joined him and a few minutes later they were being whisked up to the eighteenth floor.

'This is where you get out,' he said. 'I'm one floor above.'

Emma moistened her lips nervously. 'When you've settled in, are you returning to the clinic?'

A beautifully curved eyebrow rose, and she knew instantly he was not used to being questioned.

'It's just that I—that I want to go back there myself,' she stammered. 'I'll feel easier in my mind if I do.'

He shrugged. 'I'm having a bath, a shave and breakfast first. So if you want to come with me, be ready to leave in an hour and half.'

Emma's bedroom was the last word in luxury, and her bathroom a sybarite's dream, with mirrored walls, a shell-shaped wash basin and huge round bath with gold taps in the shape of dolphins. Finding it irresistible, she was soon soaking in its depths, and wouldn't have been surprised if a handmaiden had come in with asses' milk to pour over her!

Later, slipping into a dressing-gown, she debated between ordering breakfast in her room or going down to the coffee bar—lyrically extolled in the mass of literature she had found on her dressing table. This hotel seemed to have it all! French and Brazilian restaurants, innumerable bars, a gymnasium and sauna, and a magnificent shopping arcade.

Promising herself that at some stage she would take a quick glimpse at everything, she decided to dress and go in seach of a snack. But even as she went to pick up her bag, a knock at her door heralded the arrival of a waiter with a food trolley.

'I didn't order anything,' Emma exclaimed, and knew, even as she spoke, that Brett Adams had done so.

Pleasure at his thoughtfulness was almost instantly negated by the possibility that he might prefer her to breakfast in her room rather than bump into her in the snack bar, a situation that did not augur well for their stay here! Well, two could play the same game, and she'd make sure she found out in which restaurant he was lunching or dining so she could avoid him.

She was in the foyer ahead of time, and wandered over to the nearby bookstall. On a newspaper rack she saw a two-day-old copy of *The Times*. But strikes, Royal gossip and City news were too far removed from her now to hold her interest.

She turned to watch the people coming out of the elevators, and almost at once saw her employer emerge. He was casually dressed, but, oh, what casuals! Finest wool slacks that moulded his strong hips, and a matching brown silk sweater edged with blue, through which the muscles in his shoulders and chest rippled.

Seeing him in these surroundings was like meeting a stranger, and she tried to imagine how she would feel if he really was. That she would find him overwhelmingly good-looking went without saying, but also irritatingly sure of himself, and emanating a smouldering sensuality that any red-blooded female would long to sample!

Horrified at where her thoughts were taking her, she went over to join him, outwardly cool, inwardly in a turmoil.

Typically, he made no move to meet her half-way, watching her through half-closed lids that made it impossible for her to guess his thoughts. Not that he could harbour warm feelings towards her, she admitted, remembering the hard-hitting things she had said to him. And she wouldn't take back a single one!

'Feeling more refreshed?' he asked in an I-couldn't-care-less voice.

Nodding politely, she went with him to their car and, as before, he settled in the rear and immersed himself in his thoughts.

Painful ones too, Emma surmised, if his haunted expression was anything to go by, and knowing he was totally oblivious of her, had an excellent opportunity to study him.

Although his skin was deeply tanned, it had a silky texture, as did his hair, which today seemed a darker shade of mahogany. It was expertly layered, and she humorously acknowledged that it probably received better professional attention than her own!

In profile he appeared younger than his actual age, despite the fine lines etched round his eyes, and the deeper ones at the corner of his mouth. It was beautifully shaped, the top lip well curved, the lower fuller. Though he was clearly unhappy at the moment, the sides of his mouth still curved upwards, as if he found the world an amusing place not to be taken seriously. Was that why he diced with death and refused to be encumbered by emotion?

Yet there had been emotion in plenty in the way he had nursed Cindy throughout the flight. Certainly enough to give the lie to some of Miss Upton's allegations. But what of the other things she had said? That it wasn't death alone that had separated Cindy's parents, but that Mrs Adams had been running away from her husband when she was killed. And this, of course, could be the real reason he kept his daughter at arm's length: because she reminded him of the wife he still loved and mourned.

It might also be the reason for his obsession with racing. People often flung themselves into work as a means of coping with loss. Or had it begun before then, and was that why his wife had left him?

Emma's curiosity was so strong she was scared. Her employer's life—past, present and future—had nothing to do with her, and she must stop thinking about him.

'What did you say?' he asked.

Startled, she realised she had muttered aloud, and said the first thing that came into her head. 'I was thinking about you saying you didn't like being driven, and I—I'm surprised you haven't hired a self-drive car.'

'I'm in no mood to ward off lethal Rio traffic,' he replied. 'It's all I can do to ward you off.'

It was a split second before she got his meaning, and she couldn't help chuckling.

'That's the first time I've seen your teeth,' he said abruptly. 'Other than when you've bared them at me!'

She laughed outright. 'You make me sound awfully ferocious!'

'You are.'

'Only when I think I'm right.'

'Women always think they're right,' he said cynically, and lapsed into silence again.

Arriving at the clinic, they were told that Dr Filho, who was looking after Cindy, wished to speak to them, and they were shown to the first floor and a corner room where a soft-spoken man in his early forties came from behind a paper-littered desk to greet them.

'Cindy has viral pneumonia,' he stated without preamble, 'and the next few hours are critical.'

Emma's heart thumped loudly in her ears, but not so loudly that she didn't hear the sharp intake of breath from the man beside her.

'What are her chances, Doctor?' he asked. 'And don't give me false hope. I want the truth.'

'I understand. But it's not easy to be precise. I'd say fifty-fifty.'

'Then I'd like to stay here.'

'Of course.' Dr Filho went to the door. 'If you and your wife wish to see Cindy . . .'

'I'm the governess,' Emma said hastily as she followed the two men to a small private room filled with a frightening array of equipment.

Cindy was in a tent of transparent plastic, her eyes closed, her body inert. As they came in, a nurse moved away from the bed and spoke a few quiet words to the doctor, who then moved over to look at the child.

Brett Adams followed, laying his hand lightly on the blanket. A nerve twitched in the side of his cheek but it was the only sign of emotion he gave as he turned away.

'Daddy!'

It was the faintest of sounds but it made the man spin round. In two strides he was by the bed again, kneeling beside it to bring his face level with his daughter's.

'Hello, angel,' he said huskily. 'I thought you were asleep.'

'I—I was. Where am I?'

'In a clinic in Rio.'

'Did you come here with me?'

There was such wonder in the tremulous little voice that tears flooded Emma's eyes, and she prayed with all her heart that the man was sensitive enough to realise the implication of the question.

'Of course I came with you,' he said. 'You're Daddy's girl, and I wasn't going to let you come here alone.'

'Is Emma here too?'

'She's right behind me.'

He moved slightly, the better for Cindy to see, and Emma stepped forward.

'Hello, darling. You can't get rid of me as easily as that! I'll be staying here until you're well enough to come home.'

Cindy tried to speak, but even as her lips parted, her head turned against the pillow and her body lay still.

'God!' Brett Adams's voice was anguished. 'Is she . . .?'

'Asleep,' Dr Filho answered, his fingertips on the flaccid wrist. 'Until she saw you she was very restless. But knowing you're here . . .' He gave a slight smile. 'There's a special bond between a child and a parent that often works where medicine fails.'

'I'm afraid I haven't been all that close to her,' came the clipped response.

'It isn't the amount of time you spend with a child that matters. It's the intensity of your feelings when you're with her.'

'I didn't allow myself to show any feelings.'

Listening to the admission, Emma was filled with unexpected pity for him. It wasn't easy for a man of his temperament to make such a confession, and she knew that only guilt could have forced it from him, almost as though it were an act of expiation.

'Be that as it may,' the doctor murmured, 'your daughter now knows you love her—which is all that matters.'

Brett's head tilted sharply. 'You honestly think she does?'

'Without a doubt. Look how peacefully she's sleeping—which she wasn't until you came.'

The lean frame rose, the brown eyes glittering so brightly that Emma knew they were awash with tears.

Silently the doctor opened the door. 'There's a room at the end of the corridor where you can wait.'

'If there's any change, will you——'

'Immediately.'

For the rest of the day, Emma and Brett remained at the clinic. She had not expected a man of his vitality to sit quiet for so long, but apart from an occasional pacing he remained motionless in an armchair. Only his eyes gave away his turmoil, though she pretended unawareness of it. Her words had come home to roost with a vengeance, and she was deeply sorry for him.

Coffee and sandwiches were available whenever they wished, and every so often Brett went to look at Cindy and talk to the nurse watching her.

'Would you prefer it if I went to the hotel?' Emma asked towards the late afternoon, not sure if he would rather be alone.

'Certainly not,' he said curtly. 'I'm glad of your company.'

Since he had barely spoken a dozen words to her in as many hours, she found this hard to believe.

'I mean it, Emma,' he added. 'You're restful to have around. You know when to keep quiet, yet your silence speak volumes!'

'That's a back-handed compliment, Mr Adams, but nicer than a two-handed insult!'

He laughed for the first time that day. 'Better make it Brett. After the home truths you've flung at me, I don't think we're on Mr terms.'

He was right, yet she was wary of the familiarity it might bring. Calling him Mr Adams made it easier for her to think of him as her employer and not as a devastatingly handsome widower.

'It won't make me more likely to pounce on you,' he said, misreading her expression.

'It might make me pounce on you!' she flashed, deciding attack was her best line of defence.

'I doubt that. You've made your opinion of me all too clear.'

Embarrassed, she looked away. 'I was horribly blunt, Mr—er—Brett. I'm awfully sorry.'

'No, you aren't! Nor should you be. Everything you said was true. But let's concentrate on the future, shall we?' The grim truth of the present must have suddenly hit him, for he paled and turned away, unable to continue.

'You aren't to blame for her illness,' Emma said softly.

'I feel I am. If she'd been happier, she mightn't have caught this bug.'

'Happy people get sick too. And Cindy will get better. Dr Filho said your being with her had already made a difference to the way she was responding.'

'Thanks for the pep talk,' came the dry response. 'You're a kind girl, Emma.'

Blushing, she looked down at the magazine on her lap.

'What sort of life did you lead before you came out here?' he asked unexpectedly.

'A much duller one than this.'

'Duller? But you live like a nun in Mertola!'

'Some nun! I'm in a wonderful home with a dozen dishy men!'

'To whom you never give a second glance—other than Bill. And you keep *him* at a distance.'

She was surprised he had noticed and aware of her reaction, he raised a dark eyebrow.

'I've watched you, Emma. Waited for you to make a slip, in fact, and show me your true colours!' One lean finger rubbed the side of his cheek. 'But you disappointed me. You never flaunted yourself in a bikini when you taught Cindy in the garden, and you didn't join my crew for drinks in the evening!'

'What would you have done if I had?'

'Sent you packing. After the last disaster I employed,

I vowed I wouldn't suffer another. You'd have been out on your ear within the hour.'

'A bit arbitrary, don't you think? Would my partner in crime have been banished with me?'

Brett shook his head and her amusement decreased rapidly.

'I'd hardly call that fair,' she commented. 'It takes two to tango, you know.'

'In my experience it's usually the woman who starts the dancing!'

Recollecting those she had seen with him, she said sharply, 'Men usually get the women they're looking for!'

'Is that a crack at me?'

'Well, I——'

'You're right,' he cut in. 'In the last few years I've taken my pleasures where I found them.'

Embarrassed, she looked away. She suspected Brett's forthrightness was due to tension, and that later he would regret it.

Neither of them spoke for a while, and he was so still she thought he had fallen asleep. It was only as she went to pick up another magazine from the table that she saw his eyes were open.

'I'm surprised you can sit quiet for so long,' she said impulsively.

'I was meditating. I find it the best way to relax.'

'Did anyone teach you?'

'An Indian.'

'I can't envisage you at a guru's feet!'

'I wasn't. And he was an airline pilot! You shouldn't jump to conclusions without solid evidence,' he drawled. 'If you learned to meditate, it might help you concentrate on essentials.'

'Like you do on your pit followers?'

'They're the trappings of success—totally meaningless to me.'

'You make yourself sound very cynical.'

'Not merely sound it, my dear. I am. As I've already told you, loving a woman is the least rewarding emotion—other than in terms of sex.'

'But love's been responsible for some of man's most wonderful creations.'

'Sex has,' he contradicted. 'Once a man allows love to dictate to him, he ends up a slave to it.'

Getting to his feet he yawned and stretched his six-foot frame. Emma had always admired beauty and could make no exception of this man; he could have modelled for Michelangelo.

Feeling suddenly breathless and claustrophobic, she went to stand by the window.

'Why not go into town and browse around?' Brett suggested. 'You've seen nothing of Rio.'

'I'm not in the mood.'

'If you——' He stopped as a nurse came in. 'Cindy?' he asked instantly.

'She's awake and wants to see you.' The nurse looked at Emma. 'She asked for you, too.'

Delighted, Emma hurried after Brett. But her hope that Cindy was her old self again was dashed by sight of the inert figure in the bed.

'Feeling better, poppet?' Brett enquired gently.

'It still hurts when I breathe,' Cindy croaked, and reached out to him. 'When are you going home, Daddy?'

'Not until you're well enough to come back with me.'

A smile lit up the flushed face and she drew her father's hand to her cheek. 'I love you, Daddy.'

'And I love you.' The incisive voice had a discernible tremble as Brett touched his mouth to the damp forehead.

'Is Emma here?' Cindy whispered.

'I am, darling.' Reluctant to intrude on father and daughter, Emma had hovered by the door. But now she moved forward. 'You must hurry and get well. I'm bored without you to look after.'

'You can look after Daddy.'

'That's your job,' replied Emma brightly. From the corner of her eye she saw the nurse mouthing at her, and following the instruction said, 'I think you should rest now, darling. We'll be in to see you again soon.'

Once more they returned to the waiting-room. The afternoon ticked by, and at five-thirty Dr Filho came to tell them that Cindy's temperature had come down and she was still asleep.

'There's nothing you can do here,' he went on. 'It will be better for you to return to the hotel. If there's any change I'll call you there.'

Accepting his suggestion, they returned to the Plaza Palace. Brett did not ask Emma to join him for dinner, and as she went to her room she experienced an unexpected sense of let-down. Yet why? Although he'd been friendly to her this afternoon, it didn't mean he wanted her company the whole time. She was governess and companion to his daughter, not him, and it would be as well to remember it!

Sinking on to the bed, she tried to reassess her view of him. He was projecting a far nicer image today than when they had first met, and it was imperative she didn't succumb to his potent charm.

If she did, she might—heaven forbid—end up a racing groupie!

CHAPTER FIVE

EMMA was roused from her troubled thoughts by the telephone. Heart pounding she reached for it, relaxing as she recognised Bill's voice.

'Just calling to see how you are,' he said. 'I've spoken to Brett and he says Cindy's getting along fine.'

'She is. But she's so frail, I'm scared.'

'Don't be. Kids are tough, and this one's a fighter.'

She is now, Emma thought, remembering the way Cindy had kissed Brett's hand. 'How are things your end?' she asked.

'Quiet without the boss. What are you doing with yourself?'

'Debating whether to go down to dinner or have it sent up.'

'Go down,' Bill ordered. 'A pretty girl shouldn't hide away in her bedroom—alone, that is!'

'You racing men have one-track minds.'

'Leave out the racing,' he teased, 'and you'll be right!'

She laughed. 'Thanks for ringing and cheering me up. I'm sorry you aren't here.'

'You're only saying that because I'm miles away. If I were on the next floor you'd be locking your door—with me on the outside!'

'I suppose you think I'm stupidly old-fashioned?' she couldn't help saying.

'I think you aren't in love,' he replied. 'When you are, you won't hold back.'

His comment remained with her long after their

conversation had ended. Was he right? As she'd never been in love, she didn't know. Even the men she had known at teacher training college—many of whom had made it plain they'd be hers for the asking—had failed to turn her on, and she wondered if she had set her standards so high that she would never meet anyone who lived up to them.

'Then I'll stay single,' she said aloud. 'That's better than settling for second best.'

But was it? The prospect of living alone, of never enjoying marriage and children filled her with such dismay that to take her mind off it, she leafed through the hotel directory to see which restaurant took her fancy. Not the rooftop one, with its revolving rotunda— it was bound to be filled with couples, and parties out for a glamorous evening. A solitary diner, especially a female one, would stand out like a single rose on a thorn bush!

That left three more to choose from, and she finally plumped for the Amazon, with its promise of 'the best of Brazilian food in exotic surroundings'. It would be too bad if by some unhappy chance Brett chose the same restaurant! Yet if she found herself walking past his table, that was exactly what she'd do—walk past it! He'd never asked her to dine with him in his home, and he needn't think he was obliged to do so here. In fact, he clearly didn't!

Quickly she flipped through the dresses in her wardrobe, astonished to see so many. She had packed without thinking, dumping an armful of clothes into her case and hoping for the best. And they were definitely her best, so much so that if she remained in Rio any length of time she would have to buy some casuals.

Donning a blue silk two-piece—a favourite of hers— Emma realised she had regained some of the weight she had lost, for the material clung to her rounded curves and hand-span waist. The colour enhanced the toffee-gold of her hair, which, after several weeks of sun, was streaked with silver-gilt, an effect sought but rarely achieved by Mayfair salons. Anxiety had deepened the grey of her eyes, their colour now woodland-smoke, and she decided against eyeshadow, though she hid the pallor of tiredness with a touch of blusher, liking the way it emphasised her cheekbones.

'You'll do,' she said jauntily to her reflection, before picking up her handbag and going downstairs.

The Amazon, aptly named, was unlike anything she had imagined. It was a long narrow room set with Brazilwood chairs and tables interspersed by exotic greenery whose leaves varied from the tiny feathery to plate sized. One wall consisted entirely of glass down which a continuing stream of sparkling water poured, causing the trees and plants behind it to shimmer mistily, as they would in the jungle.

Only when she was shown to a small table inches away from the glass, did she realise that the 'jungle' which appeared to stretch for hundreds of yards behind it, was no more than three yards deep, being a brilliant combination of real vegetation and *trompe-l'oeil*.

Anticipating that as a woman on her own she would have to wait some time before being served, which happened all too often in English restaurants, she was agreeably surprised to find herself the instant centre of attention of several waiters, whose admiring eyes made it evident that an attractive-looking girl would have no problem getting service—in more ways than one!

The large menu was intimidating, despite there being an English translation, and after trying to concentrate on it, with heavy breathing around her, she asked to be left alone to make her choice.

Reluctantly two of the waiters stepped back, leaving a third hovering close by, his olive-skinned face intent on hers.

Trying her best to ignore him, she bent her head

lower to the large parchment card. All at once the prospect of eating in solitary splendour was daunting, and the spurt of spirit that had brought her here, began to fade quickly.

A shadow fell across the menu, and irritated that the waiter should be standing so close, she looked up to glare at him.

But it was Brett! The card trembled in her hand and she clenched it tighter, hoping he hadn't noticed. In a superbly cut grey silk suit that moulded the strong lines of his body, and a cream shirt so fine that the dark hair on his chest could be glimpsed through it, he was every inch the glamour personality. Small wonder that women fought for his attention. If he drove a truck they'd do the same!

'Good evening,' she said composedly. 'I didn't think you'd be eating so early.'

'Is that why you rushed down—to avoid me?'

'How could I know you'd choose the Amazon?' she came back, and the gleam in his eyes told her she had won this round, at least! She decided to press home the advantage.

'We don't dine together in your home, Mr—er—Brett, and I see no reason to impose myself on you simply because we're staying in the same hotel.'

'So your decision to eat alone was to save me the tedium of your company, and not the other way around?'

It took a second for his meaning to sink in, 'Oh, no!' she gasped. 'How could you think that?' The tilt of his mouth showed he didn't, and her wits returned. 'I assumed you had masses of friends here, and I didn't want you to feel obliged to entertain me.'

'I never feel obliged to a woman! But we're both here because of Cindy, and I'm too damn depressed to foist myself on my friends or seek out new ones. So,

since I can be myself with you, I'm more than happy
for us to share a table.'

It was hardly the most flattering of reasons—but then
it was stupid of her to think liking would motivate his
behaviour!—and she nodded and waited to see what he
would do.

'Another table, I think,' he went on, and in fluent
Portuguese proceeded to make his wish known.

Within an instant, they were settled at a larger one
further down the room, with the *maître* himself hovering
nearby to attend to them.

'Have you already ordered?' Brett asked.

'I was still floundering,' she confessed. 'Perhaps you
could choose for me . . . I know nothing about Brazilian
cuisine.'

'It's a mixture of Portuguese, Indian and West
African. Quite different from the rest of South America,
which is a blend of Spanish and Indian cooking.'

'West African? That's surprising.'

'Not if you know your history. West Africans were
once imported as slaves throughout this continent, and
Brazil's the only country where their original culture
has remained. Hence some marvellous West African
dishes.'

'You sound interested in food.'

'Cooking's a hobby of mine.'

Emma's eyebrows rose. First meditation, now cooking.
Her image of the man was fast changing, and she was
by no means sure she liked it—because she liked it too
much!

'I can't see you slaving over a hot stove,' she
murmured.

'I don't. I'm quick, capable and competent!'

'Modest too!'

'I don't believe in not knowing one's worth.'

Emma thought this over, then nodded. 'You're right.
We're actually told to love ourselves, aren't we?'

'Are we?'

'Of course. "Love thy neighbour as thyself." And if you don't love yourself . . .'

Her voice died away as she saw Brett's face harden, and instantly she knew she had put her foot in it. But in what? Some past pool of misery that was still haunting him, obviously.

'We'd better order,' she said quickly, 'or the *maître* will give up on us!'

With a visible effort Brett put aside his dark thoughts. 'Are you a health nut or do you eat meat?'

'I'm a health nut who eats meat!'

He smiled, and relaxed further. 'You mean you like the best of both worlds?'

'Naturally.' A dimple came and went in her cheek. 'And don't bother with your next comment!'

'Which is?'

'That women usually do!'

'I see you're back in fighting form, Emma, but I refuse to let you rile me while we're eating!' He perused the menu. 'The *vatapá's* excellent here. That's a mixture of shellfish and ordinary fish cooked in coconut milk and palm oil.'

'Sounds interesting.'

'And we can have *canja* to begin with—a rather special chicken soup.'

'I'll go for that too.'

'Good.' He set aside the menu. 'Do you drink wine?'

She hesitated remembering Bill had told her Brett was abstemious, and not wanting him to order a bottle especially for her.

'Well?' Brett repeated. 'Do you?'

'I'm quite happy with mineral water.'

'Which means you'd like some wine,' he drawled. 'Why the reluctance to admit it? Scared I'll think you a secret imbiber?'

'Certainly not!' Her thick silky hair bounced as she

tossed her head, and she was aware of his eyes on it. 'Only I wasn't sure if you wanted wine.'

'I enjoy it. And Brazil produces some excellent burgundies. I always make a point of having the food and wine of the country I'm in. It makes travel more interesting.'

'I suppose you travel a lot?'

'Yes.'

'Don't you ever yearn to settle in one place?'

'I'm too restless.'

Remembering his ability to relax, she felt he wasn't being wholly truthful, and wished she knew what drove him to such a peripatetic existence and continually to lay his life on the line.

The arrival of their food cut short her musing. The soup was unusual and excellent, as was the main course, which they washed down with a wine that lingered deliciously on the palate.

Brett looked pleased when she said so, and, deftly removing the label from the bottle, handed it to her.

'I believe they export it to Britain,' he commented.

'It would probably be too expensive for my pocket,' she said, setting the label on the cloth.

'But not your millionaire's—when you find him.'

'What makes you think I'm looking for one?'

'Aren't all girls?'

'How sad you should think so!'

He shrugged. 'At least one knows where one stands with them. And it's a hell of a lot simpler to give your money than yourself.'

There it was again. The cynical attitude of a man whose wife had walked out on him and their child. Yet she was unlikely to have gone for financial reasons.

'If money isn't your criterion,' he continued, 'what are you looking for in a man?'

'I'm not sure. I haven't thought about it.'

'Then do so.'

He folded his hands on the table and watched as she obeyed.

'Empathy,' she said finally, tinglingly aware of his gaze. 'I think friendship and understanding are terribly important.'

'Not sex?'

'That too.' She met his eyes without flinching. She was darned if she'd let him embarrass her. 'I don't think it's necessary to talk about it.'

'Why not? A good sexual relationship is as important as friendship. More so in fact. Without sexual compatibility, everything else could go out the window!'

'Trust you to think that! You only see women as sex objects!'

'True,' he agreed complacently. 'So maybe I'm the wrong man for you to be having this discussion with.'

'You were the one who raised the subject,' Emma reminded him. 'I'm quite happy not to talk about it.'

'That's the strange thing about you,' he mused, his warm brown eyes ranging slowly over her. 'Most of the women I know love talking about themselves, but you're secretive as a Siberian stream.'

'I don't follow that simile.'

'A frozen vein of virginal water that comes to life when hotted up!'

A bubble of laughter escaped her. Brett might be a difficult man to know, but he was definitely an amusing one.

'You should laugh more often, Emma. It makes you beautiful.'

'Now hyperbole I can appreciate!'

His face creased into a smile. What a difference it made to him: lighting his eyes, curling his mouth, removing the harsh grooves in his face, so that for the first time she had a glimpse of the man he could be if he were untouched by bitterness. He must have loved his wife very deeply to be so hurt still.

'It wasn't hyperbole,' he went on. 'You *are* beautiful. I didn't realise it until the other night when you attacked me—verbally I mean!' Again his eyes assessed her, lingering this time on the softness of her mouth and the lavender shadow of the cleft between her breasts.

Emma trembled as though he had actually touched her, and felt an incredible warmth in the pit of her stomach. This can't be happening to me, she thought. He means nothing in my life. Nothing. Yet her body was saying something different, as were her hardening nipples.

'Stop flirting with me, Brett,' she said crisply. 'I don't want to be "out on my ear with a ticket back to England".'

For an instant he didn't comprehend, then his lips curved upwards. 'I might make an exception in your case.'

'I'd rather you didn't. It wouldn't work, anyway. Emotions have a habit of getting out of hand.'

'Are you always so practical?'

'I try to be.'

'Pity,' he murmured.

Before she could answer, a waiter arrived with the sweet trolley, which she studied as assiduously as a priest the Bible.

'I can see passion takes second place to passion fruit!' he teased, and she laughed, at ease again, and glad he had accepted her decision to keep their relationship where it was.

For the rest of the meal they talked idly, and only when coffee was served did he refer to Cindy.

'You've a lot to answer for, Emma. Making me show her I love her is the last thing I wanted to do.'

'How can you say that when it's saved her life?'

'Because it will intensify her grief if anything happens to me!'

It was on the tip of Emma's tongue to remind him he could always give up racing, when she remembered the answer he had given her previously. He was an obsessed man and she had to accept it.

'Look, Brett, I agree it's dreadful to lose someone you love, but it's far worse to feel *un*loved. And until today, that's how Cindy felt. But now she knows you care for her—you saw the way she clung to you and kissed your hand—you can't take that security away.'

'I can't let her control my life either. I've reached the top of my profession because I've refused to have any emotional commitments, and that's the way I want it to remain.'

'It can't! You made a commitment to Cindy this afternoon, and if you renege on it and anything happens to her, you'll never forgive yourself.'

Brett's hands clenched on the table. 'I wish to hell I'd never listened to you! I should have kept my distance from her.'

Dismayed to be made the scapegoat for something he had done of his own volition, Emma lost her temper.

'I refuse to take the blame for something you did yourself. The moment you knew Cindy was ill, you took control. You were the one who insisted on bringing her to Rio, and you were the one who insisted on holding her throughout the journey. I had nothing to do with it.'

'You had everything to do with it. You made me feel guilty!'

'The guilt was already there! I only made you realise it.'

Abruptly he pushed back his chair. 'Let's get out of here and go to the hospital.'

Silently she followed him, appreciating the reason for his anger and knowing she wouldn't take back one single thing she had said to him.

This time a different car awaited them: a sleek Adams coupé which he drove himself, and Emma breathed in the delicate aroma of leather and rubbed her hand sensuously over the highly polished wood surface of the dashboard.

'What a fabulous car,' she commented.

'I haven't switched on the engine yet!'

'I meant the look and feel of it.'

He raised his eyes heavenward. 'Is that how women judge a car?'

'That's how men judge women!'

He flung her a wry look. 'Is catching flies your hobby?'

'Come again?'

'You enjoy taking a swipe at me!'

Her eyes crinkled with humour. 'Sorry. But you do leave yourself open.'

'Not usually. But there's something about you that makes me talk too much.' A tanned hand reached for the ignition key and the engine purred into life, smooth as silk.

'What car do you drive?' he asked as they set off along the Avenida Atlantica, in the direction of the quiet suburb where the clinic was.

'None. I don't drive.'

'You're kidding!'

'Not at all. I've no need of a car. I'm walking distance from the nursery school where I teach, and if I have to go anywhere else, there's excellent public transport.'

'What a contented girl you are.'

Emma frowned. How staid he made her sound. Yet perhaps she was. After all, what had she achieved in life?

'There's no reason to scowl,' he added, glancing her way. 'I meant it as a compliment. Contentment's a rare thing these days.'

'How contented are you?' Emma asked boldly.

'Enough to continue as I am.' There was a hard edge to his voice. 'Unfortunately, most women can't accept things as they are. They always want to change everything and everyone.'

His reply to her question answered many more unspoken ones, and she began to form a picture of what his marriage had been like. Clearly his wife had disliked his way of life and he had resisted her efforts to alter it.

'Cat got your tongue?' he demanded. 'I'm waiting for you to defend your sex.'

'I can't. Women do like changing things—something to do with the maternal instinct, I suppose.'

'That's as good an excuse as any!"

He stopped at a red light and a small saloon drew alongside him. The driver—a young man—recognised him and excitedly launched into conversation, continuing even as Brett started to pull away.

'What was he thanking you for?' Emma asked when they had finally shaken free of him.

'Nothing much. He's a motor mechanic and was talking about some of the innovations the car manufacturers are now incorporating in their models.'

'But he specifically thanked *you,*' Emma persisted. 'I understand that much Portuguese!'

'They were our ideas,' Brett said laconically. 'Put a car on a race track and you soon learn what works and what doesn't. Racing's more than a fun sport, you know. We test cars to the limit, and the knowledge we gain from it helps increase their safety. As of now, more than a dozen of our ideas have been adopted, and the royalties we get from them finances more racing and more research.'

'When you say we, I take it you mean you?'

He shook his head so vigorously that a mahogany strand fell forward, and he raked it back with an

impatient hand. 'I mean we. Racing's a team effort.
Every man has his job and every job is vital. I get the
fame—I grant you that—but without my team I'm
nothing.'

You also take the risk of being killed or hideously
injured, Emma thought, but knew better than to say it.

'I suppose Adams cars are the safest on the road,'
she murmured.

'We like to think so.'

'Your father must be proud of you.'

'It cuts both ways. He started the company on a
shoestring and we now sell worldwide.'

'Will you ever go into the firm?'

The lift of the wide shoulders could have meant
anything, though it definitely meant Brett had no
intention of committing himself!

They drove on in silence, with Emma increasingly
aware of the strong thighs only inches away from hers,
and the long-fingered hands firmly yet gently holding
the wheel.

She couldn't help wondering what they'd feel like on
her body, and angrily pushed away the thought. It was
a stupid one anyway, bearing in mind his opinion of
women. He probably took his satisfaction from them
without giving a damn if they derived any from him.
Even as she thought this, she instinctively knew it
wasn't true, for Brett was a perfectionist, and an
unsatisfied woman would be a slur on his competence
as a lover.

Her eyes slanted to his profile: the obstinate chin,
aristocratic nose, and the full lower lip which gave a
glimpse of the emotion he tried so hard to conceal.

Thankfully she saw the clinic ahead of them and was
out of the car almost before it stopped. She drew in
deep breaths of the warm night air, ridding herself of
the musky scented heat of him.

Dr Filho was in the lobby as they walked in, and came quickly across to them.

'Good news, my friend,' he said, putting a hand on Brett's arm. 'Cindy's—how do you say?—out of the wood.'

Joy suffused Brett's face, and his eyes lightened to molten gold, a gold that came, Emma realised, from the overhead light reflecting the tears he was desperately trying to keep at bay.

'Do you think I could see her?' he asked huskily.

'She may be sleeping, but by all means go up.'

Brett headed for the lift, then, seeing it wasn't there, took the stairs two at a time.

Emma stayed where she was. If Cindy was awake, far better for father and daughter to be alone together.

'You have been with Cindy long?' Dr Filho enquired.

'Only a few weeks. But it doesn't take long to love a child.'

'How true.'

They chatted on till Brett returned, his expression more content than Emma had ever seen it.

'When do you think we'll be able to take her home?' he asked the doctor.

'Not as soon as you would like! But we won't keep her a moment longer than necessary.'

Brett looked at Emma. 'Do you want to pop up and see her? She's awake.'

'I'll let her rest and see her tomorrow.'

Outside the clinic, Brett paused and looked around him, almost as if seeing his surroundings for the first time. Then, emitting a sigh, he went down the steps to his car.

They had been driving for some minutes before Emma noticed they were heading away from the hotel.

'I thought I'd take you to see a spectacular view of Rio,' he explained when she asked where they were going. 'It's a tourist "must".'

Soon they left the city behind and began steadily climbing a mountain road, the car's headlights cutting a swathe through the darkness until they finally parked high on a headland, with the city to their right.

'You'll have a better view if you get out,' he said. 'But I warn you, it's windy.'

'I don't mind.'

Opening the door, she stepped out, a gesture she instantly regretted as she was nearly blown off her feet. Her dress flew up, her hair whipped round her face, and she staggered back.

Iron hands gripped her round the waist and half-carried her along a rough path to a massive rock which acted as a bulwark against the wind. Only when she was behind it and had caught her breath, did she take notice of the view.

Brett hadn't exaggerated when he'd said it was spectacular. Myriad lights sparkled in a bowl of darkness, festooned by a glittering necklace splayed out along the city's curving coast line, while behind it loomed the mass of the Sugar Loaf Mountain, black in the moonlight, with the massive statue of Christ—spotlighted against the dark sky—spreading out its sculptured hands to bless the city beneath it.

'It's unbelievable,' she breathed. 'Thank you for bringing me.'

'My pleasure. But we'd best get back in the car. You're shivering.'

They raced back to the warm interior, where Emma attempted to smooth her dishevelled hair.

'Leave it,' he ordered. 'I like it untidy.' His eyes ranged over it. 'It's an unusual colour. Is it natural?'

'Of course!'

He chuckled at her indignance, and caught a strand between his fingers. 'It's very beautiful, and so are you.'

For what seemed an infinity, yet could only have

been seconds, they stared at one another. In the dim light she could not see the colour of his eyes, only their gleam, and she felt she was drowning in their depths, losing her senses in the warmth of him that wrapped round her like a potent charm—as his arms were now doing.

'I've been wanting to do this all evening,' he said huskily, and pressed his mouth on hers.

His touch was exactly as Emma had imagined: cool, firm, yet with a hint of fire. Desperately she forced herself not to respond, hoping he could not hear the pounding of her heart and the blood racing tumultuously in her veins. This was only a kiss, after all, a meaningless gesture from a man who treated women as playthings to be picked up and discarded at will.

'Kiss me back,' he urged upon her lips.

'Why should I?'

'You might enjoy it,' he said, barely raising his mouth from hers. 'It's worth a try!'

Not waiting for her answer, his tongue glided along her lower lip, then rested between the top and bottom one, not forcing entry, yet showing by tantalising darting movements, what he wanted to do.

Determinedly Emma kept her mouth closed, though she was increasingly aware of the sensuous pleasure of his breath on her cheek and the scent of his hard, lean body. Why am I holding back? she asked herself. It's only a meaningless kiss that we'll both forget tomorrow. And what a story I'll have to tell my children: that Brett Adams the racing champion once fancied me!

With a soft murmur she wound her arms about his neck and parted her lips. Brett muttered deep in his throat as his tongue penetrated the moist interior, the burgeoning pressure of his body showing all too clearly what her response was doing to him. Tentatively her hands explored his face, enjoying the faint roughness of stubble under her fingertips, the silky curve of an eyebrow, the velvet-soft texture of an eyelid. A tremor ran through her, beginning in the pit of her stomach and gathering intensity as it travelled lower and became a yearning ache between her thighs. How she wanted this man!

Shyness forgotten, she strained closer to him, revelling in the hardness of his chest against her soft breasts, her tongue rubbing against his, absorbing its moisture and knowing this was what she had waited for all her life.

How naïve of her not to have realised it before, not to have recognised why she had hated the girls who followed him around, and why his behaviour to Cindy had hurt her so much. From their first meeting he had sparked an antagonism in her that had been born of fear, of knowing that unless she was constantly on guard he could turn her life upside down.

So what was she doing in his arms? Hadn't he made it clear he had no time for love? For her to think otherwise was asking for heartache. Besides, he only saw her as a stop gap, the sympathetic woman he momentarily needed.

But what did *she* need? Certainly not Brett's lifestyle or profession. All he could give her was sex, and marvellous though that would undoubtedly be with him, it wasn't enough on which to build a relationship. Yet knowing this did not stop her desiring him, could not prevent her body melting against his, her lips parting wider to give him total entry.

As she did, one of his arms lifted away from her and she felt their seats tilt backwards. For an instant anger overcame desire—did he see her as some cheap lay in a car?—then she was lying flat and he was half on top of her, raining kisses on her throat, her ear lobe, the curve of her shoulder.

'Brett, no!' She struggled to rise but he wouldn't let her, the weight of him pinning her down.

'Don't fight me, Emma, I need you.'

His hand sought the curve of her breast, and at his touch her resistance faded and her body relaxed. Aware of it, he groaned deep in his throat.

'Emma,' he said thickly, and once more sought her lips.

This time she responded with a matching desire, fatefully accepting that if she didn't savour these moments she would always regret it. Hungrily his tongue probed deep inside her mouth, and she trembled with passion as she heard his murmur of pleasure.

Her entire body tingled, and the aching longing between her thighs intensified. Arching her hips, she pressed tightly against him, and he thrust her legs apart and lay inside them.

Acutely she felt the throbbing swell of his arousal and it set her alight. Moaning, she ran her hands down his spine and pressed him closer still. He stiffened, then urgently tugged her dress off her shoulders to bury his face between the fullness of her breasts. His mouth turned from side to side, gently caressing the soft roundness and taking the hardened nipples in his mouth, sucking first one, then the other, until the ache inside her grew unbearable and she longed for him to penetrate her completely.

With a suddenness that startled her, Brett drew away and sat up, at the same time returning their seats to the upright position. Then he leaned back and closed his eyes, his breathing as heavy as if he'd run a mile.

Quickly Emma did up her bra and shakily rearranged her dress. Her hands trembled and she was close to tears, still so emotionally aroused she could barely think straight.

'Thanks for not turning cold on me,' he said softly. 'I was badly in need of female warmth.'

She recoiled as though struck. Even though he had only said what she had inwardly known, to hear him state it so bluntly made their shared passion seem like a barnyard coupling!

With an effort she bit back a sharp retort, knowing it would give away her hurt, and he must never know how deeply it *did* hurt.

'You're a sweet kid,' he went on, fleetingly touching her cheek.

'I'm only eight years younger than you—not eighty!'

'But I'm aeons older in experience, my little virgin!'

In the act of fastening the last button, her hands stilled. 'How do you know I am?'

'The way you acted.'

'It could have *been* an act.'

'In which case . . .' He sent the seats falling back, and she gripped the handle of the door to keep herself upright.

'No!' she cried, and he laughed and let the seats rise again.

'Called your bluff, didn't I? You can't fool me, Emma Fielding. I don't remember when I last made such chaste love to anyone.'

Heavens! If that was chaste, what was passion? But she dared not think any further.

'I'm sorry if it was a let-down for you, Brett.'

'Now you're fishing for compliments.'

'I'm not.'

'But I'll pay you one anyway. I enjoyed kissing you.' He paused. 'Very much indeed. And with practice it would get better too.'

'My practice, I assume?'

'Our mutual practice.' He was still teasing. 'No two couples are alike, and the more you rehearse, the better the play!'

'Well, the play's over,' she said with a calm she was far from feeling. Indeed, if she followed her instincts she'd hit him on the head! Except that it would only give him a bigger laugh, and she had already amused him enough.

Smoothly he set the car in motion and they made their way silently down the mountain road and back to the hotel.

As they walked to the lift, she thought of all the other girls Brett had made love to, and felt such a desire to hurt him that it took a conscious effort not to say something spiteful.

Shaking with repressed fury, she stepped out at her floor, surprised when he followed her, took the key from her hand and walked with her to her room. Inserting it in the lock, he pushed open the door and stepped back.

'Good night, Emma,' he said softly, then touching his hand to her mouth, walked away.

The moment she was alone, Emma ran over to the mirror. Her windswept reflection stared back at her, her eyes starry, her lips faintly swollen. She touched her hands to her breasts: they were still engorged with desire, the nipples protruding stiffly, as though waiting for Brett's fingers.

She murmured his name to herself, afraid that no matter how softly she said it, he might hear. Yet even if he did, he would never guess she loved him.

Oh, God, what had she said? Weakly she sank on to the bed, wanting to pretend it was a slip of the tongue, yet knowing it wasn't. Anyway, why fool herself?

She loved Brett. Loved him as he was, loved him for what she knew he could be. But the one thing he would never be was hers!

With an anguished cry she buried her head in her hands. She must go back to England. The longer she stayed here the harder it would be to get over him. She'd hand in her notice tomorrow. Tell him her replacement at the nursery school was leaving and she had to return.

Even as she dreamed up the lie, she dismissed it. He was too astute to be fooled by any excuse she gave, and would guess her real reason—and she would die rather than let him know the truth!

It left her with no option but to stay. With luck, she'd be able to keep out of his way once Cindy was well and they returned to Mertola. Not that he'd want to see her when he was with his crew and the groupies who followed them! After all, he'd made it plain at dinner tonight that he was in no mood to look up old friends or chat up new ones, so what better than to while away the time making love to the innocent little governess who was conveniently at hand?

The mere thought of it made her squirm with embarrassment. If only she hadn't responded to him so ardently, or let him see how nearly she could have been his for the taking. Still, he'd probably put it down to his sexual prowess and not guess it was because she'd fallen for him.

Sighing, she stood up and undressed. It was impossible to alter what had happened, but she could make sure it didn't occur again. The next time Brett got the urge, he'd have to look up his little black book!

Upon which resolve, she climbed into bed and cried herself to sleep.

CHAPTER SIX

EMMA's looks did not pity her, and, going downstairs to breakfast, she appeared even younger than usual, her thick, shiny hair held away from her face by a cream silk ribbon that matched her pleated skirt and top. Glimpsing herself in the mirror lining one wall of the lift, she wryly hoped Brett would see her passionate response to him last night as the ardour of a schoolgirl!

She was on her second cup of coffee in the brightly decorated snack bar where breakfast was served when he joined her. How rested he looked. His skin glowed, his eyes gleamed, his mahogony brown hair shone. It had been no sleepless night for *him*!

'Good morning,' he smiled. 'Sleep well?'

'Yes, thanks.'

'Me too.'

'Maybe it's because last night you implied I was a tranquilliser,' she said with deliberate humour.

'An excellent one that doesn't leave me with a headache!' he responded. 'I hope you'll let me repeat it tonight?'

She poured herself a cup of coffee she did not want. 'Won't your friends be surprised if you don't contact them?'

'I'm not in the mood. And even if I were . . .' He paused, frowning, then said abruptly, 'Even if I were, I'd rather see you. I enjoy your company, Emma. You're relaxing without being boring.'

'Then I'll be delighted to have dinner with you.'

As she said it, she knew she was going completely against the decision she had made last night. But who was wise when they were in love and had a chance of being with the loved one?

'I doubt I'll get to the clinic this morning,' he said. 'I've several long-distance calls to make. But I'll take over from you after lunch so you can do some sightseeing.'

'You're determined to make a tourist of me!'

'Let's say I don't want you going home complaining you didn't see anything of Brazil.'

How casually he spoke of her return to England. It served to remind her of the difference in their emotions: his untouched, hers in turmoil.

The rest of the day passed as predicted. Cindy chatted a little to Emma, but seemed more content to be read to. She was still being carefully monitored, and doctors and nurses frequently came in to examine her, an attention she clearly enjoyed.

'You'll be thoroughly spoiled by the time you're ready to go home,' Emma teased.

'When will that be?'

'That depends on Dr Filho. A week, I should think.'

'You and Daddy won't leave me before, will you?'

'I certainly won't,' Emma replied. 'But your daddy might have to. You know how busy he is.'

'But he promised to stay with me,' Cindy said with some of her old mutiny. 'If he doesn't, I'll make a scene, like Mummy used to. She——'

'Hey, I'm in the middle of reading you a story,' Emma cut in. Despite her burgeoning curiosity about Brett's late wife, she didn't think it right to encourage Cindy to gossip.

Docilely the child settled back against her pillows, and feeling very virtuous, Emma picked up the latest episode of *Tarzana—Girl from the Wild*.

Brett didn't arrive at the clinic till three, coming in with his arms full of brightly wrapped packages which he dumped on his daughter's bed.

'Are all these for me, Daddy?'

'Unless you've a twin sister!'

Giggling, Cindy began tearing the paper, but she soon tired and left Emma to it, exclaiming with delight as one sumptuous present after another was disclosed: books, games, a painting set and a home computer. The little girl didn't know which to look at first, her attention jumping from one gift to another.

'Children are so impatient they don't understand how to enjoy the pleasurable,' Brett murmured to Emma, his eyes resting on her mouth.

Oh God, she thought desperately, what's happening to me? Don't let me love this man so much. No good can come of it. I mean nothing to him, nothing.

'Be off on your sightseeing,' his voice interrupted her reverie. 'But make sure you're back at the hotel for our dinner date.'

As if she could forget! Forcing a calm she did not feel, she kissed Cindy's cheek.

'Don't I get a kiss too?' Brett asked.

Emma smiled and tried to walk past him. But she had reckoned without Cindy, who clapped her hands and called out, 'You must kiss Daddy, you must!'

Knowing it was useless not to comply, Emma stood on tiptoe to do as she was bid, but Brett turned his face so quickly that their lips met, and the touch of his mouth remained with her as she hurried down to the car.

The driver waiting for her turned out to be a guide—how surprisingly thoughtful Brett could be—and he took her on a whistle-stop tour of the city.

Modern edifices of steel and concrete stood alongside graceful colonial buildings and evoked a more leisurely era. Wide, tree-lined avenues were interspersed with arcades of glittering shops, and wherever one turned one saw a church, though the loveliest was the São Francisco da Penitencia, its exquisite interior sculpted by hand and glittering with gold.

But it was the setting of the city, rather than the city itself, that enthralled: the huge curving bay, the limitless blue-grey ocean, and the backdrop of viridian, jungle-covered mountains.

A shortage of time made it impossible for her to see the many museums she would have enjoyed visiting, and she chose instead to go to the botanical garden, one of the best in the world, with its breathtaking avenue of palms that seemed to stretch as far as the eye could see. However it was the enormous water lillies, some of them over twenty feet in circumference, that caught Emma's eye, as did a surprising small greenhouse filled with the flesh-eating Venus fly-trap plants, which inexplicably put her in mind of the groupies that followed Brett from race track to race track!

Pushing aside the fanciful thought, she returned to the car for the mountainous drive to view the great statue of Christ atop the Sugar Loaf Mountain.

The sight of it rising immense into the sky drove everything from her mind, and her head reeled beneath the statistics her guide recited: a hundred and twenty feet high, each outstretched arm weighing thirty tons, total weight over one hundred. Close up, the detail of it predominated, and the reverence it inspired when viewed from a distance was lost.

Emma couldn't help likening this to her emotional response to Brett.

As long as she had viewed him from afar she had been able to regard him with detachment. But seeing him in the intimacy of a close, everyday relationship, she had begun to see the emotional conflicts warring

within him which, in turn, had given her a better
understanding of him, an understanding that had
finally led her to love him. All too cognisant of the
heartache this would bring her, she knew that the
sooner she left him the better.

The sun was sinking below the horizon as she
returned to the city, and mindful of the travel books
she had read before coming here, Emma asked to
see the slums—*favelas*, they were called—a pretty
sounding name for a shaming eyesore of a shanty
town of tin and wooden shacks, with no sanitation or
running water, and no roads. Yet this was home to
nearly twenty-five per cent of Rio's population, and
though many of them worked in beautiful houses and
hotels, it was to this cesspit they returned each night.

She was still deeply disturbed by it as she walked
into her hotel. The glamour and glitter of the vast
lobby seemed somehow obscene, as did the well-
dressed tourists around her. Yet she was intelligent
enough to accept that no individual group could
eradicate the horror she had seen. It was a world
problem, and would have to be tackled as such.

It made her own emotional problems seem totally
insignificant, and the realisation helped her view her
future with a greater sense of equanimity.

Why shouldn't she enjoy the pleasure of the
moment without worrying about the morrow? It was
not an attitude that would last, she knew—she was
too logical to believe that—but if it helped see her
through this bittersweet evening, she would be
grateful.

She was in the act of picking up her bag to go
down to meet Brett when a bellboy arrived with a
spray of tawny tiger-lillies.

Pleasure warred with dismay as she regarded them,
for beautiful though they were, their colour clashed
with her Italian print dress. Hastily she changed it for

a wisp of pleated beige crêpe, a lucky buy in last
year's summer sale that, because of her mother's
illness, she had had no chance to wear.

She had decided against doing so tonight because it
was too dressy and she hadn't wanted Brett to think
she was getting dolled up for him, but short of an
uninspiring cotton she now had no option, and
carefully zipping up the crêpe, she attached the
flowers to one slender shoulder strap.

The glint in Brett's eyes as he saw her emerge from
the lift, did much for her ego, and she gave him a
confident smile.

'I assume you believe in the language of flowers?'
she asked.

'Clever of you to guess! I immediately discarded
the thought of violets, and it was a toss up between
tiger-lilies and passion flowers!'

She blushed, and the widening of his grin showed
an awareness of it as he guided her out.

The restaurant he took her to was on the coast, a
few miles from Rio. Many of the diners recognised
him as he entered, and the head waiter led them to
the best-positioned table overlooking the white sandy
beach, and presented them with a bottle of champagne
with the compliments of the house.

Very much aware of being the centre of all eyes,
Emma nervously unfolded her napkin.

'Perhaps we should have gone somewhere more
obscure,' Brett remarked, noticing her shyness.

'No matter where we'd gone, someone would have
recognised you. Anyone connected with cars and
horses seems to become a universal celebrity!'

'Thanks,' Brett said drily. 'You're really turning my
head!'

'Sorry,' she laughed, and sipped her champagne.

Half-way through the meal, which she again left
Brett to choose, he drew her on to the dance floor.

Conscious of the many eyes on them, Emma tensed and stumbled.

'I'm not used to being stared at,' she apologised.

'Forget it and concentrate on me!'

That was likely to make her even more tense! But she dared not say so, and forced herself to ignore the other dancers. Gradually she felt herself relax, and Brett's hand tightened around her waist.

'That's better,' he murmured. 'You dance as well as you kiss.'

'You're trying to make me nervous again!'

'Nervous at the thought of kissing me?'

'Why should that surprise you? You're a famous man, Brett, with the world at your feet and umpteen mistresses on the sidelines!'

'Ouch! I'm glad I decided on tiger-lillies. You enjoy hitting below the belt, don't you?'

'Don't tell me it hurt you?' she mocked.

'A blow to my heart,' he replied, lowering his lips to her hair as the music changed to a slower tempo.

Emma's heart pounded heavily and she had difficulty breathing. But whether it was Brett's closeness or the warmth of the atmosphere, she didn't know.

'I'm sorry,' she gasped, 'but I—I don't feel well.'

Instantly he drew her off the floor and propelled her out to the terrace, where tables and easy chairs had been set.

Emma sank into one and closed her eyes.

'Breathe slowly and deeply,' Brett advised her. 'You downed the champagne too quickly and it's gone to your head.'

'Probably because I've had no food to absorb it,' she murmured. 'I missed out on lunch.'

'Why?'

'Cindy didn't want me to leave her.' Emma felt better in the air, and opening her eyes, saw Brett leaning back in his chair.

It gave her another view of him, showing her the firm line of his jaw and the strong throat. Yet despite his physical strength, he was vulnerable, and she had a vision of him spread-eagled on the ground, limbs crumpled, or worse still, the centre of a blazing fire. She gasped, experiencing the pain of it, and Brett leaned towards her quickly.

'Feeling worse?'

'No, no. Much better, in fact.'

'Good. You know, you shouldn't let Cindy boss you around.'

'She doesn't. But she's still far from well, and I didn't want to upset her by leaving her and going out to lunch.'

'You love her, don't you?'

'I love most children.'

'And adults?'

'Some. Generally they're not very lovable.'

'Am I?' he asked, bringing his face close to hers.

'When you take the trouble.'

'I want to take a lot of trouble with you,' he whispered, and rested his mouth on hers before gently pulling her to her feet. 'Let's finish dinner,' he said unsteadily. 'I don't think I'll have any more champagne either. You're intoxicating enough.'

Knowing he was flirting with her, but not wishing to shatter this lovely moment, which might be the only one she would have of him, she let him hold her hand as they returned to their table to finish their meal.

'I'm surprised a beautiful girl like you isn't married,' he commented as they were sipping their coffee.

'I'm only twenty-three. I want to do much more with my life before I tie myself down.'

'I was two years younger than you when I married.'

'That *is* young for a man.'

'Any age is too young for a man! Especially in my profession.'

'Why?'

'Because it's a lousy life for a wife, particularly when the children come along. It means she has to leave them behind if she wants to be with her husband.'

'But racing doesn't go on all year, does it?'

'Six months of it, sometimes more. And even if a wife elects to stay home, she eventually starts nagging her husband to change his profession.'

'How many wives succeed?' Emma couldn't refrain from asking.

'Only a small percentage.'

She could well believe it, for racing seemed to require a degree of obsession, and an obsession was difficult to give up.

'But why are we talking about racing?' Brett demanded. 'I'd much rather talk about *you.*'

'You're far more interesting,' she protested. 'A man of many parts and many moods.'

'No sports writer would agree with you. Don't you know they call me Robot Adams? Apt, don't you think?'

'Not any more.'

'Then you're kidding yourself. I'm a tough bastard, Emma, make no mistake about it.'

'Not as tough as you think. You've kept your emotions locked up—I realise that now—but yesterday Cindy turned the key.'

'I'll re-lock it,' he vowed.

'Your feelings for Cindy won't let you.'

He shook his head. 'If I could hold firm against Eileen—my wife—I can do the same with my daughter.'

'Hold firm?'

'To do as I want. Eileen made my life hell because I wouldn't quit racing.'

'That's different. If you didn't want to give in to her, I can understand it.'

'Can you?'

'Certainly. She at least knew your profession when she married you!'

'What's that got to do with it?' he asked cynically. 'Don't you know what your sex is like, Emma? As your mistress, a woman will take you as you are and profess herself delighted. But once she's your wife, she sets about changing you!'

Emma wondered if she'd do the same if she were married to Brett, or if she could accept that he was laying his life on the line every time he climbed into his racing car. It was an appalling thought, and she did not even begin to know the answer.

Their return journey was a silent one, giving her time to ponder on what she had learned about the unknown Eileen, and wishing she could draw Brett out on the subject. But remembering he'd called her an inquisitor only two days ago, she held her tongue.

'You're very quiet,' he remarked.

'You don't like idle chatter.'

'That doesn't usually stop a woman!'

'Poor Brett. You do seem to be unlucky with the girls you meet.'

'Either that, or you're cleverer than most.'

'Cleverer?'

'At pretending.'

Emma was stung by his comment. 'At the risk of repeating myself, I think you're a lousy judge of character.'

'Sorry,' he said instantly. 'I shouldn't let out my cynicism on you.'

They drew up at the entrance to the hotel, and left the car to be parked by one of the attendants.

'I may have to fly back to Mertola for a few days,' Brett informed her as they entered the lobby. 'But I'll be back to bring Cindy home.'

'She'll be upset at your leaving.'

'Will you?'

'You haven't gone yet.'

His eyes gleamed. 'Hazard an answer.'

'Of course I'll miss you,' she replied sedately.

'That goes for me too,' he said, holding out his hand to the desk clerk for their keys, and receiving them together with a message slip.

'Bill wants me to ring him,' he frowned. 'I wonder what's up? I only spoke to him a few hours ago.'

'Maybe your cars are missing you!'

Brett was still chuckling at this as she stepped out of the lift at her floor, bidding him such a firm good night that he took the hint not to accompany her to her door.

'You won't always escape me,' he called softly after her.

But I'll have a damned good try, she thought as she reached her room. Tonight had been an evening stolen from time, one she would remember for the rest of her life, but one it would be wiser not to repeat if she valued her peace of mind.

Charming though he had been to her, it was only charm, and she'd be foolish to think otherwise. Brett could take his pick of women, and she meant no more to him than an amusing incident.

But for her it was the exact opposite, and from now on she must make it clear she didn't want to see him socially. He'd probably think she was childish, might even be angry with her. But that was somethign she'd have to accept.

Indeed, anything was easier to accept than falling more deeply under his spell.

CHAPTER SEVEN

THE moment Emma saw Brett next day, she knew something was wrong. The light flecks in his eyes seemed paler, more yellow than brown, and there was a tight set to his jaw that boded ill for someone. Whatever it was Bill had told him last night, it hadn't been pleasant.

She learned what it was as he led her into a small side lounge, and irritably paced the carpet.

'Eileen's parents and sister are in Rio. They tried to get me at Mertola last night—which was why Bill called me—to tell me where they were staying.'

'It's lucky you're here,' Emma murmured cautiously.

'Bad luck,' he corrected, making no pretence at simulation. 'I don't get on with the Proctors. I never have.'

'Have you spoken to them yet?'

'Yes. They thought they'd combine a vacation with seeing Cindy. "Our darling granddaughter,"' he quoted with a sneer. 'Ever since Eileen's death they've been pressurising me to let Cindy live with them.'

Two days ago it would have struck Emma as a good idea, and even now, bearing in mind he still intended sending his daughter to boarding-school, it might be the best solution.

'If I read your expression correctly,' Brett said drily, 'then the answer's, "No, it wouldn't".'

'Why not?'

'Because the only reason they want her is that she'd be a meal ticket for them.'

'I don't follow you.'

'You're too innocent! If anything happens to me, Cindy's my sole beneficiary, and though it's all in trust, her guardians, whoever they were, would get a substantial allowance for bringing her up. Which accounts for my in-laws' desire to have her.'

'But if anything—I mean——'Emma stopped, embarrassed, and Brett shrugged.

'If anything happens to me, Cindy will stay at boarding-school and spend her vacations with my father.'

'Aren't you being rather hard on the Proctors? They're family, after all, and——'

'Blood's thicker than water?' he finished angrily. 'If that's what you think, there's no point discussing it.'

'At the moment it's a Brett Adams monologue, not a discussion,' Emma said spiritedly. 'At least clarify your dislike of the Proctors so I can form my own opinion.'

'You'll be able to do your own clarifying in half an hour. When Bill told them where I was staying, they said they'd book in here as and from today.'

'Do they know Cindy's been ill?'

'Bill told them that too.'

Emma was dismayed Brett hadn't thought to do so himself. No matter how much he disliked his in-laws, they had a right to know.

'Don't judge me until you've met them,' he said perceptively. 'If you still think I'm overly critical, I've no doubt you'll tell me!' Upon which he turned on his heels and left her.

Sighing, Emma went to her room to catch up on some of her correspondence.

The imminent arrival of the Proctors had made Brett revert to the cynic she had first met, and she intuitively knew that his dislike of them stemmed from more than their desire to look after Cindy. Was it because the very thought of them reinforced the guilt he felt at his broken marriage? A guilt that could well have been increased by his wife's death? How she wished she knew the whole story!

Emma was on her third letter when Brett telephoned to ask her, in a tone that brooked no argument, to join him on the roof terrace.

Reluctantly she did, nervous at the prospect of meeting his parents-in-law, and found them at a shaded table overlooking the swimming pool. They were an elderly, well-dressed couple as she had expected, but she was startled by the beauty of their daughter, a younger, brunette version of Brett's late wife.

He made the introductions, and pulled out a chair for Emma to sit beside him. Hardly had she done so when a waiter arrived with coffee. Brett made no attempt to pour and since the Proctors didn't either, she was obliged to play hostess. Irritated by Brett's ungracious behaviour, she gave him a sharp look, which he met with one so bland that she knew it to be an act.

'I still think Cindy should live with us in England when she's well again,' Mrs Proctor continued the conversation Emma's arrival had obviously interrupted. She was thin and tall, with a lined but still good-looking face, marred by a razor-thin mouth.

'I don't agree,' Brett replied coldly. 'She's very happy at Mertola.'

'While *you're* there,' Mr Proctor put in. He was a mirror image of his wife, and could easily have passed for her twin brother. 'But how happy is she when you're away and she's left in the care of strangers?'

'She doesn't regard Emma as a stranger,' Brett said

silkily, and instantly three pairs of eyes focused on her.

'Don't you think my granddaughter would be happier in a more temperate climate?' Mrs Proctor questioned Emma.

'She seems to thrive in the heat.'

'This happens to be the Brazilian winter! In their summer it's unbearable.'

'Which is why I'm sending her to boarding-school in England,' Brett stated.

'She's too young for boarding-school,' his mother-in-law exclaimed. 'If you don't want to take responsibility for her yourself, why won't you let her live with us? I don't understand how you can be so hard towards us. She's our only grandchild and we love her.'

Brett said nothing, and as the silence lengthened into one of awkwardness, Emma turned to Brett's sister-in-law. Close up, she was not as lovely as she had seemed at first glance, her eyes being set too close together and faintly foxy.

'Is this your first visit to Brazil?' she asked.

'I was here three years ago, when Eileen was alive.'

'Then you know Mertola.'

'What there is of it.' The girl regarded Emma from eyes as glacial a blue as her mother's. 'Aren't you bored to death there?'

'Oh, no, I love it. The scenery's beautiful.'

'So are the Romney Marshes. But no one in their right mind would want to live there!'

Hastily Emma changed the subject. 'How long are you staying in Brazil?'

'I'm not sure. Probably a month.'

Emma glanced at Brett. He had heard their conversation and favoured his sister-in-law with a cold look.

'Since you dislike Mertola so much, I won't invite you for a visit! Rio's much more your scene.'

'We aren't here for a holiday, you know,' Mrs Proctor intervened. 'We came solely to see Cindy. I couldn't believe it when Bill told us how ill she'd been, and that you hadn't seen fit to let us know.'

'It only happened two days ago, and there seemed no point worrying you when you were so far away. Besides, there wasn't anything you could have done.'

'We could have flown here at once—just to be with her! Really, Brett, you're sometimes so heartless. Don't you understand Cindy's our only link with Eileen?' Mrs Proctor dabbed at her eyes with a handkerchief. 'I still can't believe she's dead. She was so young and full of life. If you'd been more understanding with her, she——'

'I don't want to discuss my marriage!' Brett set his cup sharply on the table. 'Raking up the past won't help anyone! And if seeing me brings back painful memories for you, you'd have done better to stay away.' Pushing back his chair, he stood up. 'If you want to see Cindy, we'd better go. She gets tired quickly and sleeps a lot.'

'As long as we see her for a few minutes we'll be satisfied.' Mrs Proctor rose too. She was unusually tall, and wore her elegant clothes with considerably more panache than her husband, who was ultra-conservative in slacks and dark blazer. 'It might be best if you don't come with us today, Diana,' she said to her daughter.

'OK,' Diana shrugged, as her parents moved off with Brett, who gave Emma no sign of wanting her to go with him.

What a man! she thought crossly. Did he expect her to stay and entertain his sister-in-law? Somehow she thought not, for Diana Proctor, slim and elegant

as her mother, looked more than capable of taking
care of herself.

'How long have you been with Brett?' the girl
asked.

'Seven weeks.'

'That's quite a while to be flavour of the month in
Brett's life!'

It took a second for Emma to realise the implication
and she was hard put to keep her temper.

'I'm Cindy's governess, as you've already been
told, and I'll be escorting her to school in England.'

'You don't look the governess type.'

'I'm a nursery school teacher, but I took a six
months' sabbatical.'

'Not much of one!' came the amused response.
'From what I remember of Cindy, she's an impossible
child.'

'I find her very easy.'

Emma sprang to Cindy's defence like a lion
defending its cub, and Diana shrugged again and
signalled a passing waiter for more coffee. Emma
tried to leave, but a small, surprisingly firm hand
stopped her.

'Don't go. I hate being alone.'

'I don't think we've any more to say to each other.'

'Oh dear, you're annoyed because I thought you
were Brett's latest. But I didn't mean to be rude. It's
simply that you're a pretty girl and I assumed . . .
Well, I'm sure you know Brett's rackety lifestyle, and
why one tends to think that any girl living in his home
is part of it.'

'Mr Adams's home life is extremely circumspect,'
Emma said stiffly.

'What there is of it! He's more away than at home
and Cindy hardly sees him. He was like that when
Eileen was alive and I know he hasn't changed.'

'He's a very caring father,' Emma asserted, thinking firmly of the present.

'Come off it! He's a handsome bastard who doesn't give a damn about anyone except himself.' Diana paused and let out a sigh. 'I dare say I shouldn't be talking to you like this, but how would *you* feel towards the man who'd caused your sister's death?'

Emma's hands shook and she quickly clasped them in her lap. 'I'd rather not discuss my employer, if you don't mind.'

'He *did* cause her death, you know,' Diana went on remorselessly. 'She'd be alive today if he'd been half-way decent as a husband. That's why we want Cindy to live with us—to get her away from his influence.'

Had Diana said this several days ago, Emma might have agreed with her. But not now, not since seeing Brett cradle his child in his arms, his whole bearing grief-stricken.

Yet he was still going to send her away to school, had even thought of reverting to his earlier aloof position! But that wasn't because he didn't love his daughter, Emma reasoned, only that he loved racing more.

'I know Brett's furious with us for coming here,' Diana continued. 'But that's because he's still scared we'll spill the beans about him. It wouldn't do his image much good if the public knew he was little short of a murderer!'

'I really can't listen to this!' Emma exploded.

'But you should if you care about Cindy's well-being. He killed Eileen as surely as if he himself had crashed the plane in which she was flying.'

'That's a terrible thing to say!'

'But true. Once Eileen accepted that Brett didn't give a damn about her, hated her in fact, she knew she couldn't live with him.' Tears filled the blue eyes. 'You never knew my sister so you can't begin to understand what she was like. But she was stunningly beautiful, and so full of vitality that when she walked into a room everything glowed into life. That's why Brett fell for her, of course. From the minute he met her, he pursued her non-stop.'

Each word was like a dagger in Emma's heart, and she tried to resist the pain. Eileen Adams was dead and it was wrong to be jealous of her.

'I'd rather you didn't say any more,' she whispered.

'I remember Eileen walking round on cloud nine,' Diana went on as though she had not heard. 'Not that it took her long to come crashing down, though.' The oval face grew pointed as an indrawn breath formed hollows beneath the cheekbones. 'That was when Brett first walked out on her. My God, we thought she'd kill herself!'

'But—but didn't your sister leave *him*?'

'That was years later, after they were married. I'm going back to when they were engaged. Brett suddenly decided he no longer fancied her, and left.'

'There's no crime in that.'

'When your fiancée's expecting your baby?'

Emma could not hide her shock. Living with someone and leaving them was one thing, but leaving when they were carrying your child!

'But they finally married,' she said stiffly.

'It was either that or some pretty bloody publicity for him. At first he wanted Eileen to have an abortion, and when she wouldn't he offered her a fortune to go away somewhere quiet and leave him alone. It wasn't until my parents threatened to make the whole thing public that he agreed to do the decent thing.'

All this was giving Emma a new slant on Brett's marriage, and though it lessened her jealousy to know he hadn't loved Eileen, it showed him in a light that was far from favourable. Of course he might simply have wanted an affair, and Eileen could deliberately have fallen pregnant to force his hand, in which case neither of them was blameless.

'Mind you, I think my sister was out of her head to marry him,' Diana Proctor continued. 'But she thought that once the baby was born he'd settle down. What a laugh! He carried on as if he weren't even married. Left her alone for weeks on end—and even when he was home, took no notice of her or the child.'

Emma's heart sank. What could she say to this?

'Your sister is dead, Miss Proctor. Resurrecting the past won't do any good.'

'It just reminds us to keep fighting for Cindy.'

'But he loves her! He was demented when she was ill.'

'Guilty conscience!'

'Whatever the reason, he——'

'He knew how much Eileen hated him racing,' Diana burst out, 'yet he refused to give it up. I honestly think he enjoyed making her suffer. And eventually, of course, she couldn't stand the strain and left him.'

'She left Cindy too,' Emma couldn't resist saying.

'Out of desperation,' Diana defended. 'She thought that if he was forced to take care of his child, he'd come to his senses. But it made no difference to his lifestyle. He still——'

'Please, Miss Proctor, I don't want to be involved in your family's fight with Mr Adams. Now, if you'll excuse me . . .' Emma rose and walked swiftly away, not slackening her step until she was out of the hotel.

Aflame with temper, Emma had walked a quarter of a mile along the esplanade before she became aware of the perspiration trickling down her face. Only then did she pause to wipe it and take stock of her surroundings— the blaze of white sand, the shimmer of blue-grey sea and the expanse of white-hot sky. She must be crazy marching along in this heat!

Slowly she retraced her steps, wishing she could

forget everything Diana had said. Yet her accusations against Brett could not be dismissed, for it was all too easy to visualise Eileen sitting alone night after night while Brett hit the high spots with his racing friends. This was plainly the life he enjoyed, and though he had been more than circumspect these past few days, she would be foolish to see it as anything other than the behaviour of an anxious father.

The blast of cold air that greeted her as she returned to the hotel was a welcome relief, and she wandered down to the lower lobby to look at the shops—all highly expensive, as befitted their location, and way out of the pocket of a working girl. But she feasted her eyes on the lovely clothes, and the magnificent emeralds and aquamarines displayed in the jewellers, thinking what fun it would be to go prospecting for the semi-precious stones that could be found in the hinterland.

'Well, well,' an amused male voice drawled behind her. 'So you're a normal woman after all!'

Startled, she swung round to see Brett, one hand in the pocket of his jacket, the other holding a small package.

'Normal?' she queried.

'Looking goggle-eyed into a jeweller's window! I didn't expect it from a chaste young governess who doesn't smoke, drink spirits, or hanker for a car!'

'What a daft thing to say!' Emma was more irritated than amused, and he was quick to see it.

'Diana made your hackles rise?' he asked keenly.

'She could raise the hackles on a fur coat!' Emma retorted, and Brett flung back his head and laughed.

'Sorry I had to leave you to her tender mercies,' he apologised when he could speak.

'You didn't even give it a thought!'

'I'm afraid you're right. Sorry.'

She shrugged. 'It's merely that I came to Rio to be with Cindy, and I feel I'm not doing my duty if——'

'Nonsense! She's getting all the attention she needs, so if you're anxious to take care of someone, look in my direction!' He swung the package in his hand. 'Why the glint in those lovely eyes? They're the colour of storm clouds.'

'Don't flirt with me, Mr Adams,' she said crisply.

'Mr Adams is it? Hmm, Diana *has* been talking!'

'Surely you expected it?'

'Yes. But I didn't expect you to take notice of her!'

Emma flushed, knowing his criticism was justified. After all, he was her employer and she owed him a degree of loyalty, certainly enough to give him the benefit of the doubt.

Even as she thought this, she realised Brett had told her very little of his marriage. Not that this meant Diana had been speaking the truth. Indeed, the girl was clearly prejudiced and it would be advisable to take what she said with a good pinch of salt.

'You're right, Brett. I owe you an apology,' Emma admitted.

'Forget it. Join me for coffee, will you? I want to talk to you.'

Wondering what was on his mind, she followed him to the coffee shop that overlooked a luxuriant shaded garden set with tables and chairs.

'Do you want to sit outside?' he asked.

'It's cooler in.'

He nodded and sat down opposite her. He seemed strangely on edge, fidgeting with the small package he had been carrying and which she took to be toiletries, for it bore the name of the hotel drug store. There was definitely something on his mind, but since he always accused her of jumping to conclusions about him, she was determined not to do so on this occasion.

'The Proctors want Cindy, as you know,' he said abruptly. 'And if I go on racing they could well get her.'

'Aren't you being unnecessarily pessimistic?' Emma said, despite this being her own attitude.

'Coming from you,' he mocked, 'I find the question surprising.'

'You're the one who's surprising,' she countered. 'This morning you gave me the impression Cindy's future was cut and dried.'

'It's what I thought until I saw my in-laws this morning. But they've made it quite clear that if anything happened to me they'd go all out to get custody of her. And I think they'd succeed. My father's too old to take care of a young child, and my brother's still single.'

'You could always give up racing,' Emma said.

'Maybe—when the right woman comes along.'

The words were those she longed to hear, yet his look and tone told her he didn't mean them.

'I can't ever see you content with one woman,' she remarked lightly.

'Don't you think a leopard can change its spots?'

'Even if it had stripes it would still be a leopard!'

'Pity you said that,' he drawled. 'You're making it damned difficult for me to say what I'd planned. But I'm going to anyway.' Pushing the package aside he leaned across the table. 'Will you marry me, Emma?'

Blankly she stared at him. Was this Brett's idea of a joke? But his eyes were narrow and intense, showing her that though his question was unexpected, he meant it. She moistened her lips.

'Why—er—why do you want to marry me?'

'Why do you think?'

The implausible idea that he might love her flashed into her mind, but she instantly dismissed it as romantic fantasy and plumped for logic.

'Because of the Proctors, I suppose. If I were your wife and—and you were . . . Well, I—I'd be Cindy's legal guardian.'

'That's quite true,' he said slowly.

His acknowledgement of this, even though she had expected it, was none the less painful, but pride enabled her to hide it as she said, 'But why me? You must know loads of women.'

'I do. But you care for Cindy and I know she's deeply attached to you. Well, Emma, what's it to be? Or do you find the idea too abhorrent even to consider?'

'Not abhorrent, Brett, merely incomprehensible. I know you weren't happy with your wife, and . . .' Embarrassed, she stopped.

'Don't worry about saying it,' Brett replied. 'I knew Diana wouldn't be able to resist filling you in on all the gory details, and I'm sure the way I treated Eileen figured very largely in what she said.'

'It did, but—but even if most of it's untrue, you still saw marriage as a trap, didn't you?'

'Yes. But with you it would be different.'

'Because I don't love you, and you know I won't make demands on you?' she forced herself to say.

'That's it in a nutshell.' His voice was flat, emotionless. 'So what's your answer? Most girls would jump at the chance, you know.'

'I'm not most girls.'

'Which is why I've proposed.'

'And which is why my answer is no. I can't tie myself to a man who sees marriage as an insurance policy against death! If you care for Cindy's future you should start thinking about your own.'

'Cut out the lecture,' he stormed, and before she could say anything else, he stood up and strode away.'

His abrupt departure astounded her, and even as he disappeared through the swing doors, she ran after him. The lobby was crowded and she weaved in and out among the throng, not losing sight of him yet not getting nearer either. He reached the front exit and she saw him stride down the steps, then cross the road.

In that instant there was a screech of brakes followed

by a tremendous crash. With horrified eyes Emma saw the commissionaire and two bellhops dash into the roadway. Positive that Brett had been injured, she rushed the remaining yards to the exit. A large crowd clustered on the steps and wildly she tried to push her way through.

'Please . . . let me pass,' she gasped. 'I must see him . . . please.'

'For God's sake, Emma! There's nothing you can do!' a deep voice said, and strong arms lifted her bodily clear of the throng.

Dazedly she found herself on the pavement, staring up into Brett's face. The relief of seeing him alive was so great that her vision blurred.

'You're safe,' she whispered. 'I thought you'd been run over.'

'Only by you! You banged into me but didn't even know I was there.'

'I saw you crossing the road, then heard the crash and . . .'

She shuddered, and unable to stop herself, dropped her head on his chest. She heard the pounding of his heart, slow, steady, and all at once knew that no matter what he said, no matter how he lived, she could not bear to be parted from him. For better or worse, she loved him. It wasn't a love she had sought but nor was it a love she could change. All she could do was accept it and be with him for as long as he needed her.

'I *will* marry you,' she whispered.

'Because you thought I'd been killed and you were able to envisage Cindy living with Proctors?' he asked drily.

'Something like that,' she lied, and self-consciously moved away from him. 'Anyway, it won't be for ever, will it? When you eventually give up racing you won't need me as insurance and I'll be free to—to . . .' her voice trailed away and she turned and walked towards the hotel.

'I'm glad you're seeing things logically,' Brett said beside her. 'If I settle for a desk job sooner rather than later, you'll have your freedom earlier than you expected.' He put his hand on her arm. 'Shall we have that coffee after all?'

'I'd rather go and see Cindy.'

'OK. I'll see you this evening then. I'm afraid we'll have to dine with the Proctors.'

'Oh, lord!' Emma was dismayed. 'Diana will think me a two-faced bitch for not telling her I was engaged to you!'

'Since I'm sure she started maligning me the instant my back was turned, you can always claim you didn't have a chance to do so!'

As that was exactly what had happened, Emma couldn't help smiling, and he remained in a good humour for the rest of the day. She had omitted to ask Brett when they were going to tell Cindy they were getting married, and knew without conceit that the child would be overjoyed, a fact that in no small way helped her to be sanguine about the new path she was taking.

That was more than could be said of the Proctors, whom Brett told of his impending marriage as they all sat in the outside bar, where the soft rush of passing cars behind the hotel wall mingled with the soft rush of the distant sea.

'Getting married?' Mrs Proctor was astonished. 'But you never said a word about it this morning!'

'It didn't seen appropriate.'

Brett spoke in a far gentler tone to his in-laws than Emma had heard him use before. Obviously, knowing his marriage would thwart them of Cindy made him able to curb his dislike of them.

She eyed the Proctors surreptitiously. They were not

particularly likeable, yet they didn't merit the antagonism Brett felt, and she couldn't help wondering if his attitude came from knowing they blamed him for their daughter's death.

'You must have really enjoyed yourself with me this morning,' Diana Proctor spoke softly to Emma.

'No more than you,' Emma answered coolly. 'You were so happy maligning Brett, I thought I'd let you go on having fun!'

'I don't take back a single word I said. He's a bastard—as you'll find out for yourself.'

Emma's reply was forestalled by the arrival of a magnum of champagne, and watching it being poured she was angry with Brett for ordering it. It was hard to expect the Proctors to celebrate the fact that another woman was replacing their daughter in his life, particularly since it put paid to their hopes of having their granddaughter live with them.

All at once she felt extremely sorry for Mrs Proctor. Everything Diana had said this morning could well have been a distortion of the truth, yet so might Brett's opinion of his in-laws! How difficult it was to discover the true situation when strong emotions were involved and one could only glean bits and pieces of information from both sides.

'To the future,' Brett said, breaking into her thoughts, and Emma picked up her glass and drank, conscious of being watched and weighed up, and aware that a five-foot-three toffee-blonde in an obviously off-the-peg dress from a chain-store was a far cry from the beautiful, sophisticated Eileen.

Yet despite the woman's beauty she had not held Brett's love, and Emma wondered what her own chances were of winning it. Stranger things had happened, and if a cat could look at a queen, then a chaste governess might even yet insinuate herself into the heart of a playboy.

'Will you be giving up racing?' Mrs Proctor asked, setting her glass down on the table with a sharp click.

'Why should I?' Brett drawled. 'Emma's happy to take me as I am.'

'Aren't you afraid for him?' This second question was addressed to Emma who, knowing it to be a loaded one, was careful how she replied.

'I think it's wrong to marry someone in the hope of changing them, Mrs Proctor. You either take them as they are or you don't take them at all.'

'How sensible of you,' the woman said without sincerity. 'I hope you'll be able to maintain that attitude.'

'I wouldn't bet on it,' Diana put in waspishly, looking directly at Brett. 'I see this marriage ending up the way your first one did.'

'I don't,' Brett retorted. 'Emma's devoted to Cindy.'

'Meaning Eileen wasn't?' Mrs Proctor rushed in, her voice high. 'That's a wicked thing to say! If you——'

'Margaret, please!' Mr Proctor put a warning hand on his wife's arm. 'Raking up the past serves no purpose.'

'Particularly when you don't know it all,' Brett added in clipped tones. 'And to avoid further argument I suggest we stop looking backwards and concentrate on the future. Cindy's your grandchild and I realise you love her and want to see her, but I won't allow you to if you blacken my name to her.'

'We'd never do such a thing!' Mrs Proctor said vehemently.

'I'm glad to hear it. Now what say we finish the champagne and go in to dinner?'

It was not an evening Emma cared to remember. Although the Proctors set out to be friendly, she sensed their dislike of her and could understand it. Brett acted as if he was unaware of any undercurrents, though the occasional flicker of a nerve at the corner of his mouth showed he was under more strain than he let appear.

Emma tried to imagine what it would be like married to him, then knew her life would be little different from what it was today. She would still be looking after Cindy, and Brett would carry on in his own sweet way. After all, that was why he was marrying her: so he could live his own life without having to worry about his daughter's future. Knowing this filled her with bitterness, until she reminded herself she had accepted his proposal with her eyes wide open.

Yet despite this, as he escorted her to her room when the long, uncomfortable evening thankfully drew to a close, she could not help saying something of what she had been thinking.

'Any time you want your freedom, Brett, you just have to tell me.'

'Won't I have my freedom as your husband?' he smiled. 'You aren't going to be a demanding wife, I hope?'

'You know I'm not. But I was thinking that one day you might fall in love and want a genuine marriage.'

'That's what I'll have with you, little Emma. You're as genuine as they come.'

'Thank you,' she said sedately, 'but that wasn't what I meant.'

'It wasn't what I meant, either,' he said, stepping into the lift with her. 'I know you're only marrying me because of Cindy, and I'm grateful to you for it.' His lean, tanned hand lightly stroked her cheek. 'Maybe marriage without love has a better chance of succeeding. Emotion can distort one's intelligence, you know.'

Emma stared into his face, aware that the smile on it did not reach his eyes, which remained dark and brooding.

'You're happy, aren't you, Brett?' she asked impulsively.

'As happy as I'll ever be.'

'Try not to feel guilty about your wife.'

'I don't and I never have. I did nothing I regret except——' He stopped abruptly as they reached Emma's floor and he stepped out with her.

'Why the hell are we talking about Eileen,' he muttered. 'I want to forget her.' Taking the key from Emma's hand he unlocked the door. 'Am I allowed in for a good night kiss?'

'I'll give you one here.' Raising herself on tiptoe she touched her lips to his cheek, drawing away as his head turned to find her mouth.

'Scared of me?' he asked.

'Only if you want me to be.'

Her answer made him frown.

'No, I don't. You've a kind heart, Emma, and I don't want you to be frightened of me—ever.'

Placing a soft kiss on her brow, he gently pushed her into her room, whispered good night, and closed the door behind her.

She stood beside it listening to the soft tread of his steps as they receded, knowing that he took her heart with him and that she would never be able to give it to any other man.

CHAPTER EIGHT

BRETT insisted they be married as soon as possible, and
since Emma had no family to invite, she agreed.

'Won't your father and brother expect to be invited?'
she couldn't help enquiring.

'I'll write and say you wouldn't go to bed with me
until you had a ring on your finger, and as I can't
wait——'

'You wouldn't!' she burst out.

'No I wouldn't, he laughed. 'I'll just cable and say
I'm getting married and will soon be bringing you to
England to meet them.'

Emma longed to ask if he intended letting them in
on the truth when he did, but she still felt nervous of
questioning Brett. Truth to tell, she could not evisage
ever being totally at ease with him. Yet nor could she
live on a knife edge, and it was imperative she and
Brett develop a friendship—if nothing else.

Almost as if he picked up her thoughts, he said
quietly, 'Don't be swayed by other people's opinions of
me, Emma. Judge me for yourself.'

'I've already done too much judging,' she confessed
ruefully.

'I can't disagree with you there! So why not relax
and take things as they come?'

It was good advice, but she was not sure she could
follow it yet. Brett had only to look at her for her
knees to turn to water, had only to touch her for her
body to tremble. It was nerve-racking to be so aware of
a man, so dependent on him for your happiness. She

131

tried not to think what would happen when Brett
eventually retired from racing. He would have no need
of her then, and she would have to make a life away
from him. But that could be years away yet, and she
would heed Brett's advice and enjoy each day as it
came.

The Proctors left Rio after a week, during which
time Emma did her best to avoid them. Appreciating
their desire to be with Cindy, she stayed away from the
clinic, a fact which they were too thick-skinned to
acknowledge. The more she saw of them the less she
liked them, but knowing their feelings for Brett might
have coloured their attitude towards her, she knew it
was wrong to form any hard and fast opinion of them.
As to the story Diana had told her of Brett's marriage,
well, that was something she couldn't assess either, and
it would do her no good to dwell on it.

The morning Brett accompanied his in-laws to the
airport, Emma went to the clinic to tell Cindy she
would be marrying her father.

'You, Emma?' the little girl screamed with delight.
'That's super-duper-sensational!'

'I thought you'd be pleased,' Emma said, straight-
faced.

'I'm the pleasedest in the world!' Cindy cried. 'And
now I won't have to go away to boarding-school. Not
now I've a mummy to look after me.'

Emma swallowed hard. This was an aspect she had
not considered, and she determined to discuss it with
Brett as soon as possible.

'I haven't given her schooling another thought,' he
admitted when she did. 'But now Cindy's mentioned
it . . .'

'There's no need for her to go away, is there? I'm
qualified to teach her for the next few years, and by
then . . .' Emma almost said, 'By then you may have

decided to give up racing and settle down to a normal life,' but managed to bite back the words.

However she had reckoned without Brett's intuition, for he said testily, 'I'm not marrying you to have another Eileen round my neck! So no sighs and hints as to what you think I should do with my life.'

'I wasn't hinting! It's just that when I think of Cindy——'

'Think only of Cindy,' he cut in, 'but leave *me* alone.'

Red-cheeked, she nodded, recollecting the proverb 'Least said, soonest mended'. A proverb she must religiously follow if she wished Brett to be happy with her.

'Incidentally,' he said, breaking into her thoughts, 'we'll be getting married early next week. I've had a word with the British Consul and it's all arranged.'

'N-next week?' she stammered. 'I didn't th-think it would be so soon.'

'As Macbeth said, "If it were done when 'tis done, then t'were well it were done quickly."'

Brett leaned back in his chair, his eyes ranging slowly over her as if taking an inventory. Emma felt the colour creep into her face and wished she knew what he was thinking. But a glance at his mobile mouth, the full lower lip moving sensuously, told her it was better she didn't, and she was glad they were in a crowded restaurant and not alone in his car!

'You'd better get a wedding ring,' he pronounced. 'A diamond one if you like. Go to the jeweller's in the hotel, and have them charge it to me.'

Emma nodded, hiding her disappointment that he wasn't getting it himself. But that was the romantic coming out in her and Brett was nothing if not logical. As far as he was concerned their marriage was a business arrangement and it mattered little which partner bought the ring.

Next morning an envelope with an unprecedented amount of Brazilian money—more than she earned in a year—was delivered to her room, together with a note from Brett enjoining her to buy some clothes. Although Emma knew she should be pleased by his thoughtfulness, she considered it high-handed of him to have taken this particular way of asking her to replenish her wardrobe, and penning him a short letter refusing the gift, she put the note and money into an envelope and left it for him at the reception desk.

She did not see him again until later that evening, when she met him in the hotel's roof restaurant, where their table afforded them a magnificent view of the city. He made no reference to her letter, nor did she, and they enjoyed their meal together, chatting as easily as if they were the oldest of good friends.

Despite his suggestion of the night before that she buy a diamond wedding ring, she had chosen a narrow gold one, the simplest she could find, and as she handed it to him she wasn't helped to see his look of irritation.

'I can see you're going to be a problem to me, Emma,' he said. 'First you return the money I sent you, and now you buy this—this curtain ring!'

'Can you see me wearing diamonds, Brett?'

'I can see any woman with diamonds,' he said testily. 'Your refusal to spend my money is stupid and one of false pride. And diamonds apart, all brides like to have a trousseau.'

'I'm not a bride in the real sense of the word. And if you don't like my taste in clothes . . .'

'I'm not even aware of your clothes,' he said exasperatedly. 'But other people will be once you're my wife, and either you play the part properly or not at all.'

Her eyes widened at the implication of this, and he bit back a sigh. 'Not the way you mean, damn it! Don't look so scared. There's no shortage of beautiful women around who are more than happy to warm my bed.'

'Must you be so crude?'

Surprisingly he laughed, his good humour restored. 'What an odd mixture you are, Emma. One minute old-fashioned, the next responding passionately in the car.'

Emma had been waiting for him to refer to that night, and was glad she had prepared her defence.

'I've never said I'm frigid, Brett, and you're good-looking enough to turn any normal girl's head. But we're marrying because of Cindy and it would be a mistake to forget it.'

'It might make things easier for us if our marriage was a more normal one,' he commented blandly.

'I think not.' Though angered by his assumption that she was there for the taking, she managed to hide it. 'It's more important we be good friends than bad lovers.'

'Falling back on Oscar Wilde?' he commented. 'Anyway, what makes you think we'd be bad lovers?'

'Because sex without love is meaningless to me.'

'Then we'll stick to friendship. And now that's decided, I'm sure you'll understand if I don't linger over coffee. I don't fancy wasting the entire evening!'

Hiding her humiliation, Emma gave an amused smile. She'd have to get used to Brett doing this, but, oh, how painful it was going to be!

The following Tuesday an excited Cindy was discharged from the clinic and, later in the day, was witness to her father's marriage to Emma.

With a ring on her finger and thin arms clasping her neck tight, Emma knew that come what may she would always feel responsible for this little girl, as she would always love the man standing beside her.

It was only as they left the Consul's office to face a battery of cameras that she realised being Brett's wife meant living part of their life in a goldfish bowl. It was one Brett was used to, for he parried the newsmen's questions with ease, giving quotable answers that still managed to give away nothing of his private feelings.

'I should have realised we couldn't keep our marriage secret,' he muttered as they ran the gamut of flashlights and more questions on the way to their car. 'I expressly told the Consul's secretary to make sure no one knew I was getting married today.'

'I thought publicity was important to you.'

'As a racing driver, yes, but not in my private life.'

'It's hard for a public figure to separate the two.'

'Hard but not impossible,' Brett grunted. 'If I'd thought of it, we could have been married in Embira.'

'With all your crew trailing after us?' she teased.

'You've a point there, little Emma.'

'Not so much of the little if you don't mind.' She was irritated at being talked to like a child, even though she knew it was safer if he did.

'Sorry,' he apologised, 'but in that pink get-up you could be Cindy's sister, not her stepmother!' He gave the pleated silk dress and jacket a keener glance. 'New, isn't it?'

'Yes.'

'And bought with your own money, to show your independence!'

'I—er—I'll spend yours now I'm your—now we're married.'

'The word you can't bring yourself to say is wife,' Brett stated. 'You must get used to it.'

'Give me time.'

'Poor Emma.' His tone was unexpectedly tender as he glanced at her over Cindy's head. 'I suppose you feel I've cheated you out of a proper white wedding with a dozen bridesmaids and a church ceremony.'

'I can think of nothing worse than having a dozen bridesmaids,' she rejoined crisply, her momentary mood of self-pity lifting. 'As for a church wedding—well, that's something I can have when I——' Abruptly she stopped, and again Brett finished the sentence for her.

'When you make your vows and mean them?'

'Yes. Now, may we change the subject? I'm feeling rather emotional and I'm sure you won't want me bursting into tears.'

'Do women always cry when they're happy?' Cindy piped up, reminding Emma that little pitchers have big ears.

'I rather think they do,' Emma answered brightly. 'You'll probably cry on your your wedding day.'

'I'm never going to get married,' came the confident answer. 'I'm going to live with you and Daddy for ever.'

'Well, at least until you're eleven,' Brett corrected. 'After that you may go to boarding-school.'

Cindy's mouth fell open as she absorbed what her father had said. Then she went mad with joy, flinging her arms round his neck so that the car swerved and he had to push her none too gently away, and hugging Emma and laughing and crying at the same time.

'You mean I'm not going away to school at Easter? Oh, Daddy, that's wonderful.'

Emma thought so too and the look she flung Brett said so, for he smiled smugly, the yellow flecks in his eyes more pronounced, giving them a tigerish quality.

'I knew you'd be pleased,' he said answering Cindy but looking at Emma. 'It's a present for my bride.'

'The nicest you could have given me,' Emma said huskily, and repeated this when they returned to the hotel to finalise their packing and return to Mertola.

'I always take your advice when I think it's right!' he conceded. 'And in this case it was. Depending how things go between us, I may not even send her away at all.'

Emma dared not look that far ahead, knowing that

only by living on a day-to-day basis could she hide her love for this man. Hide too her fear of what might happen to him, a fear that would no doubt intensify as each big race loomed up on the calendar.

'Have you told everyone at Mertola that we're married?' she asked as they boarded the Brazilian Airways jet that was taking them home.

'I told Bill and asked him to pass it on.'

Emma wondered how long it would take Brett's team to realise his marriage was one of convenience only, a thought that made her feel distinctly edgy as, in the late afternoon, they entered the flower-filled living-room of his home.

The men were all on their best behaviour, though this loosened up as champagne flowed, and Cindy's departure for bed loosened tongues still further.

As the ribald comments flew, Emma pretended not to hear. This was the way the team were, and her marriage to Brett wouldn't change them. Any adjustments that needed to be made would have to come from her, a fact which, for the first time, made her acknowledge that the new path she was treading might be stonier than she had thought.

Yet maybe not quite so stony, for when the men had tactfully disappeared, leaving her and Brett to dine alone, he apologised for some of their outrageous remarks.

'They aren't used to the presence of a lady, I'm afraid. I'll see they curb their tongues in future.'

'They won't be seeing all that much of me,' she said quickly. 'I'll be with Cindy most of the time.'

'And Cindy will be with me most of the time—when I'm not racing. Which means you and I will be together. I've no desire for our marriage to become a subject of gossip, Emma. I've had my fill of wagging tongues!'

His statement answered the question that had been looming in her mind since returning to the villa, and she now had her answer. Brett hoped the outside world would think their marriage was real, and though one part of her rejoiced, the other was fearful.

'It won't change anything between us,' he added, 'so don't worry on that score.'

'I'm not. Though I have my doubts about our fooling people who live so close to us.'

'The occasional affectionate look and touch will go a long way to allay suspicion.'

'Even though we'll have separate rooms?'

'Brazilian staff expect the English to be eccentric! It's only when we're back home that we'll have to be careful.'

Emma was puzzled. 'But we *are* home.'

'I mean Yorkshire. We'll be going there for Christmas.'

'I hadn't realised.'

'There's a lot you haven't realised.'

'That applies to you too.'

In the act of pouring himself a nightcap at the drinks tray, he turned to look at her across the room. 'Care to explain yourself?'

'Only that all this talk about pretending our marriage is real isn't going to work. You've already said you don't intend changing your lifestyle, and since I don't intend being an object of pity when your men see you going out with other women——'

'Why not wait till that happens?' he cut across her. 'You still haven't learned not to rush your fences, have you? I may surprise you by being a stay-at-home husband.'

'When you're racing round the world for more than six months of the year?'

'I can still be faithful to my lovely bride!'

'And pigs can fly!'

'So can people, little Emma. I intend taking you and

Cindy around with me. That's one advantage of having a governess for a wife!'

'You mean you'd like us to travel with you?'

'Wouldn't you like that?'

'Very much. But I thought . . . well, you never took your wife with you and——'

'*You're* my wife now,' he cut in, and Emma sighed, knowing she didn't feel she was, and wondering if she ever would. It was hard to feel like a wife when your husband didn't love you and would turn to another woman when he wanted passion. Aware of what this would mean if she travelled with him, could she stand aside and watch him take his pleasures elsewhere? The very idea nauseated her.

'If Cindy and I went with you,' she said aloud, 'I'd expect you to maintain the façade of our marriage.'

'You mean be faithful?'

'At least not to flaunt it when you aren't.'

'I'll be the soul of discretion,' he drawled, giving her a salute with his glass.

Quickly she turned her eyes away from his, all too aware of the handsome picture he made. He was not in his usual casual attire, but elegant suede pants and a cambric shirt of the same golden colour as the flecks in his eyes, making Emma regret she had chosen a simple blue cotton instead of something more glamorous.

'You don't look like a bride on her first evening at home.' Brett's statement echoed her thoughts. 'Did you do it on purpose?'

'Yes. I—er—I thought that if I—er—'

'Wore something glamorous I'd lunge at you with unrestrained lust?'

'Maybe. I know I'm not the Venus de Milo, but I don't look like the back of a bus either, and you do have a low threshold of resistance!'

His look was distinctly sour. 'Not so low that I'd make advances to someone who didn't want me.'

Emma was hard put not to say she wanted him very much, and tried to imagine what he'd do if she did. Probably bed her this very instant and go on doing so until he tired of her. It might give her several months of sensual delight, but also years of misery as she tried to forget it.

'Relax,' he said into the silence. 'I'm perfectly happy treating you like a sister. Though if you should change your mind . . .'

The easy smile that accompanied this showed her how lightly he'd regard making love to her, and though she was tempted to answer him back in his own terms, she refrained, knowing how dangerous this kind of word play could be. Brett was a past master at the art of flirting, but she wasn't, and could end up taking him seriously.

Yet deep down lay the hope that the more he saw of her the more she would infiltrate his mind, and that one day he'd come to care for her. Not an all-encompassing love perhaps, but an affectionate one based on friendship and shared love for Cindy. But this lay in the future; no one changed overnight, least of all Brett.

'Why the smile?' he asked.

Parrying the question with a shrug, she wandered over to the stereo to choose a record.

As the overture to *Don Giovanni* resounded in the room, Brett gave a contented sigh and sat down, nursing his drink and letting the beautiful notes wash over him.

'Mozart's my favourtie composer,' he murmured as it came to an end.

'Mine too, though Beethoven's a pretty close second.'

'I agree. Looks like we've more in common than I thought.'

'You've never thought,' she said provocatively. 'At

least not where I'm concerned. I was Cindy's governess and part of the furniture.'

'A very neat and comfortable little armchair,' he grinned.

'And you're a straight-backed, rigid monk's bench!'

'Never a monk,' he corrected, chuckling as he saw the colour rush into her cheeks. 'You're so innocent, Emma, it provokes me into teasing you.'

'Don't you like innocence?'

'I'm not sure. In children, yes, but in a woman—in a wife—I prefer maturity.'

'Does being innocent preclude that?'

'A good question.' The pursing of his mouth indicated surprise, as if it was something he'd never considered. 'I'll answer it when I've known you longer.'

That evening set the tone for their relationship, and in the succeeding weeks a rapport was established between them that gave Emma a growing sense of contentment. She wondered if Brett felt the same but he gave no sign of it, and it was left to Bill to provide her with a clue.

'It's a pity Brett didn't meet you years ago,' he commented, coming on to the verandah late one afternoon while Emma was relaxing there, Cindy having gone for a swim in the pool with her father. 'He's so much easier to work for these days. More relaxed than I've ever see him.'

'Because he's relieved about Cindy's future.'

Emma made no pretence that the change in Brett could have been caused by love, for she knew that Bill, as his closest friend, had been told the real reason for their marriage.

'It isn't relief over Cindy that's keeping him home nights,' Bill went on. 'He hasn't been out one evening with the boys.'

'I should think not! He's still acting the part of the newly-wed.'

'There's more to it than that.'

'You're wrong,' Emma said firmly, unwilling to give herself false hope.

'Wrong about what?'

This from Brett, who had strolled on the veranda to join them, his hair still wet from his swim, most of his tanned body exposed by the brief shorts that were his only covering.

'We were discussing speed and road safety,' Bill lied with commendable swiftness. 'Emma thinks all motorways should have a fifty-mile speed limit like the Americans.'

'I don't disagree,' Brett replied. 'And talking of speed, Martin agrees with the modification I've suggested on the car.'

'Great!' Bill looked delighted. 'I'll make arrangements to have it shipped home.'

He ambled off, and Brett dropped down into a nearby chair and stretched out his long legs. Sensing she was watching him, he fidgeted slightly but didn't look at her, then rested his head on the back of the chair and closed his eyes.

What had he been like eight years ago when he had married Eileen? she mused. He was so much in control of himself now it was hard to think of him as a madcap young man running away from his responsibilities, as Diana Proctor had said. The intervening years must have changed him greatly, not only giving strength to his character but also caution, for the Brett of today was unlikely to get an unmarried girl pregnant, and even if he did, would never be forced into a shot-gun marriage.

Jealousy of all the women he had known flared up in her, and she longed to hit out at him, to let him see her as the warm-hearted girl she was and not the cool, unruffled governess he believed her to be.

Stifling a sigh, she decided to go in search of Cindy

and was walking past Brett's chair when, still with his eyes closed, he reached out and caught hold of her skirt.

'Where are you rushing off to?'

'Your daughter.'

'The father needs you too.'

Emma's heart thumped, but her voice was casual as she said, 'Needs me for what?'

'Company. Relaxation.'

'Yours but to command,' she smiled and, as he let go of her dress, sat down again.

'That's better,' he said, without lifting his lids, and lay quiet again.

Once more Emma watched him, and as a moment ticked by, saw his fingers curl back as relaxation gave way to sleep. Even then she did not leave him. He had asked her to stay and she would. But then she would do anything he asked if he phrased it the right way. Which made her the prime sucker of all time, she acknowledged ruefully, for once Brett started racing again he'd have no need of her. It was only because he was bored that he bothered with her.

It was a bitter realisation, but she knew it was one she should write out and stick on to her bedhead. Only by seeing it day after day would she stop herself turning to putty that he could mould any way he wished. She went on looking at him, her love so deep that his proximity was a torture. She longed to kneel beside him, to stroke his strong hands and unruly hair. She wanted to kiss his face and lie in his arms. She wanted . . .

Unable to bear the agony, she quietly rose and tiptoed away.

CHAPTER NINE

ALTHOUGH Emma had not anticipated finding much difference between living in Brett's house as his governess and then as his wife, events proved her wrong

He expected her to be far more visible than previously, and either joined her and Cindy for lunch in the nursery or had it with them on the terrace. Though he invariably left them to their own devices morning and afternoon, once Cindy was settled for the night he insisted Emma join him again, and though to begin with they had dined with the men, this gradually became less than a nightly affair, and more often than not they dined *à deux*.

To begin with Emma found it a strain making conversation, but the more she got to know Brett the easier she found it. And he in turn was more at ease with her, which was reflected not only in what he said, but in his more easy-going attitude.

'Daddy's very happy married to you,' Cindy said one afternoon as she and Emma sat in the shade of a tree. They had worked assiduously all morning and were now taking a well-earned rest.

'I'm very happy married to your daddy,' Emma responded carefully.

'And I'm happy 'cos I've a proper mummy who won't go away.'

'I'll never do that,' Emma assured her, and unable to resist the desire to hug her close, did so and then danced with her across the grass.

'May I call you mummy?' Cindy asked as they finally flopped down again.

'Emma isn't old enough to be your mother,' Brett said behind them, and Emma felt a stab of pain at his words.

'I suppose you think it was wrong of me to say that,' he demanded as Cindy raced off to play with her ball.

'You set the rules,' Emma replied lightly.

'I didn't think you'd like her calling you mother. You're so young it doesn't seem appropriate.'

'I'm old enough actually to be her mother,' she said waspishly, 'even though you keep seeing me as a child bride!'

'OK, OK,' he caved in. 'You and Cindy settle it between you. I don't care either way.'

In the end it was Cindy who settled it, running back to throw the ball at them and shouting, 'Catch it, Emma!'

'See what I mean?' Brett commented as his daughter ran off again. 'The problem's resolved itself.'

'It was never a problem. It could only have been one if——' She stopped, embarrassed, and Brett's head tilted questioningly.

'If what?'

'If our—if our marriage had been a real one and we had children. They'd call me mummy and Cindy would feel left out of it. But as that won't arise with us . . .'

'How can you be sure? You're a lovely-looking woman—see, I no longer think of you as a girl!—and I no longer enjoy racketing around.'

As a compliment it was not world shattering, and she had no wish to be made love to simply because she was available.

'Pity you didn't think this way when you were married to Eileen,' she snapped.

'How the hell do you know what I thought then? I've told you before not to judge me, nor to take the Proctors' word as gospel.'

'I wouldn't, if you were more open with me.'

'I don't believe in the confessional. Our marriage is a business arrangement and——'

'Then why suggest it might be something different?'

He looked discomfited, and she pressed home her advantage.

'At least be consistent in your attitude to me, Brett. You married me to give Cindy another guardian, which is why I agreed to your proposal in the first place. But there's where it ends'

'You're happy to go on like this?'

'Yes,' she lied, not wishing him to make love to her simply because she was his wife. 'We entered into a contract and it's unfair of you to try to change it.'

'You're right.' His voice was brisk. 'I'm glad you put me in my place, Emma. I deserved it.'

She wished he liked her enough not to give in so quickly, and felt terriby dejected that he didn't. Her throat tightened and tears were not far away. As she struggled to hold them back, Cindy made a rush at her father and he caught her in his arms and swung her high. The child's shrieks of delight helped Emma gain control of herself, and she was able to watch with cool amusement as father and daughter romped on the grass together before he declared himself worn out and announced he was going for a gentle stroll.

'Come with me, Emma,' he said, and realising he wished to talk to her, she fell into step beside him.

For several moments they walked in silence, and only as they breasted the knoll and saw the coast ahead of them, did he speak.

'You've no need to be afraid of me, Emma. You're very attractive and I won't deny I fancy you! But I know when I'm not wanted and I'm not angry with you for sticking to the letter of our agreement.'

'It's an agreement you can break any time you like, Brett.'

'You mean——?'

'No, not that,' she cut in. 'Merely that if you wish to end the marriage . . .'

'I don't. This arrangement suits me fine.'

But for how long? she asked herself for the umpteenth time, and was no nearer finding an answer than before.

'I hope you won't mind spending Christmas in Yorkshire with my family?' Brett broke into her reverie. 'We've a big old house on the moors so we won't have to live in each other's pockets.'

'Christmas in Yorkshire sounds lovely. Do you have log fires?'

'For nine months of the year!' he grinned. 'We've central heating too, but Dad loves what he calls "real" warmth.'

'Does he know the truth about us?'

'No. It's not something I felt like discussing on the telephone and—well, I'd rather not enlighten him, if you don't mind.'

She did not know what to say to this and decided to wait and see if things became awkward when she was in her father-in-law's home.

'When are we leaving here?' she asked.

'Would a week from today suit you?'

'Depends what I have to do. Do we shut this house or will the servants stay on?'

'Until now they've stayed on, but I'm not sure what I'll be doing in the future.'

He paused, deep in thought, and though Emma longed to ask what other plans he had in mind, she resisted it.

'For the moment I'll leave things as they are,' he

continued. 'Which means you'll only have to pack your things and Cindy's.'

Emma turned to look back at the house and could not restrain a sigh. 'I'll miss this place. It's so peaceful and tranquil. On the other hand,' she added with a smile, 'a big, old house on the Yorkshire moors sounds very homely and Victorian.'

'How sentimental you are,' Brett grinned. 'You're still a child at heart, Emma, and I envy you.'

His expression became morose, and Emma guessed he was thinking of his youthful marriage and the years it had sapped.

'Forget the past, Brett.'

'I'm trying to. But it isn't easy.'

His eyes ranged over her face, and before she could anticipate his action, he leaned forward and pressed his mouth on hers. It was a kiss of unexpected fierceness, almost of anger, and he put his arms around her and pulled her roughly against him.

Emma knew he desired her, and her defences began to crumble as his kisses deepened and grew more intimate. She tried not to respond but his tongue was a flame in her mouth, rousing her to a heat that burned away reason and turned her into a quivering mass of need that could only be assuaged by pressing her body closer and closer to his, by running her fingers through his thick hair and down the back of his neck, by feeling the strong muscles in his back, the hardness of his thighs, the burgeoning swell that spoke of his arousal.

This was Brett, her husband, and loving him as she did, it seemed crazy to hold back. Perhaps if she gave herself to him he'd start loving her in return. She moaned deep in her throat, and taking it as acquiescence he drew her down behind a cluster of thick bushes that hid them from prying eyes, then swiftly unbuttoned her dress. The wisp of bra she wore was no barrier to his questing hands or mouth, and he caressed and fondled her breasts until they grew heavy and hard, the rosy nipples darkening and enlarging as he explored them with his avid tongue.

The warm air was gentle on her body, and Brett lifted slightly away to look at her. Without embarrassment she lay before him, her face soft and seductive, her thighs aching to receive him. With trembling fingers she unbuttoned his shirt, splaying her hands against the thick matt of hair on his chest before lowering them to undo the buckle around his slacks. It loosened and fell away, and as her hands moved lower still he shuddered and pressed down upon her, making her hand prisoner between them.

'Don't!' he rasped. 'If you touch me I won't answer for what will happen.'

His words, implying the need for control, acted on her like a douche of cold water, and her desire for him drained away, leaving her deeply embarrassed and defenceless—he must never know how defenceless. Only by playing it cool could she retain her pride, and she was desperately thinking what to say when he pre-empted her.

'Thanks for not going coy on me, Emma. I desperately needed to hold someone just now, and if you'd pushed me away I . . . but you didn't and—and thank you.'

'Don't make a habit of it, though,' she said, taking her cue from him.

'I won't. I value your friendship too much to have you turn against me.'

Knowing this was the only compliment she could expect from him, she fastened her bra and reached for her dress. Brett sat up and half-turned away from her, giving her a view of his profile, the eyes hooded and half-closed, the mouth relaxed yet faintly cynical.

'These past few years have been a hell of a strain,'

he muttered. 'You need to hype yourself up in order to give your best, and then you have to find ways of bringing yourself down again so you can release the tension inside you. Drink's the obvious way, but it plays havoc with your reflexes. Women are the next best solution, but, oh, how boring they can be! Beautiful bodies that slake your need, yet don't satisfy you, so that you go on searching, searching!'

'Is that what you're still doing?' Emma asked quietly, wishing with all her heart that he could turn to her with love and let her meet his needs. But knowing he could only offer passion, she fought against the urge to comfort him, knowing she had to go on playing the role of friend and confidante, and that in his own tormented way he needed her as much as Cindy did.

'God knows why I'm burdening you with my problems!' he said angrily. 'I've relaxed too long and it's made me maudlin. Once I start racing again things will be different.'

'You mean things will be the same?'

'The same? No, Emma, each day brings its own problems, and I'm just beginning to face up to mine.'

'Don't ever let *me* be a problem to you, Brett.' Emma did up the last button on her dress, and with her body covered, felt she had covered her emotions too. 'As I said before, I'm ready to go whenever you say the word.'

'What a one you are for harping on the same thing!' he chided, pulling her to her feet. 'You and Cindy are the two stable factors in my life, and I'm not about to change them.'

Happy to hear this, she let him lead her back to the house, trying not to face the fact that the longer she remained with him, the greater the pain she would eventually have to bear.

CHAPTER TEN

It was a bleak day in early December when Emma had her first sight of the house where Brett had been born. A square, solid manor of grey Yorkshire stone, it nestled in a curve of the moors, protected from the winds by a gently rising hill thickly covered with trees. The front aspect was open and inviting, the mullioned windows aglow with rosy light, the paintwork white as snow.

Inside, it was large without being rambling, though there were odd little passages that were a constant surprise to the eye, making the house seem older than its hundred years. It had all the modern conveniences though with efficient plumbing and heating, though the latter did not preclude, of course, Brett's father's favourite log fires in the main living-rooms.

Emma had been nervous of meeting her father-in-law, but the instant she did, her fears vanished, for he was an older edition of Brett, his hair more silver than mahogany, though the twinkling brown eyes had the same yellow flecks in them and the features, though wind-roughened, were as patrician. Only his voice was different, lighter than his son's, and with a pronounced Yorkshire accent.

Leaving Brett to talk privately with his father, Emma took Cindy upstairs to the rooms that had been prepared for them. The little girl had a suite on the top floor, its dormer windows looking out on a fairytale scene of hoar-frosted trees glittering in the pale, watery sunshine.

These rooms, two bedrooms, bathroom and large playroom, had obviously been Brett's and his brother's, for children's books were still neatly stacked on the shelves, and a vast toy cupboard was filled with games and toys from another era. No Space Invaders and Star Wars weapons here, but cowboy and Red Indian games, rifles instead of rockets!

A young Yorkshire girl came in, introduced herself as Millie Dodds and said she'd come to help Emma get settled, which she did by promptly starting to unpack Cindy's clothes. As she put them away, she cheerily informed her that until a year ago she had worked in a shop in Harrogate but much preferred this job.

'What other help is there?' Emma asked.

'There's Mrs Ebson and her husband Frank,' Millie said. 'She's the cook-housekeeper, and Frank does the buttling and any odd jobs that need doing. Then we've two women who come in from the village each day to help with the cleaning.'

'It sounds very luxurious,' Emma smiled.

'Well, Mr Adams does a fair amount of business entertaining. Sometimes we've as many as twenty to dinner.' Millie put a pile of blouses into a drawer and straightened. 'Like me to give you a hand with your unpacking, Mrs Adams?'

Declining the offer with thanks, and leaving Millie to explore the toy cupboard with Cindy, Emma went down to her room on the floor below. It was large and opulent, with a carpet of muted pattern underfoot and flowered brocade curtains at windows, which gave on to the same view as Cindy's. The furniture was solid and dark, the most predominant piece being a four-poster bed, its wooden poles ornately carved.

Emma bounced happily up and down on it, then

quickly stopped in case it was antique and fragile. But closer inspection showed the mattress to be new and well sprung.

It did not take her long to unpack, for she had far fewer clothes than Cindy, and knew she'd have to make a trip to her own home to collect her winter ones. Except that Brett might not consider them suitable. He had surprised her by having an excellent eye for fashion, and because of her reluctance to spend his money, he had taken her shopping in Embira himself, imperiously ordering any outfit that took his fancy.

All of them were lovely, but none of them were warm, and after emptying her cases, she slipped a cardigan over her blue and purple Ungaro dress and went to join Brett and his father in the library. The older man was still sitting in front of the fire, but Brett was in a far corner of the room playing Monopoly with Cindy.

'She's a different child from the one I saw six months ago,' Mr Adams commented as Emma came to sit beside him. 'She's so much more at ease with her father.'

'Because she knows he loves her.' Emma tilted her head to listen to Cindy's chatter. 'All you need do to make her happy is not to interrupt her when she's talking!'

Mr Adams chuckled. 'She takes after my younger son, then! By the way, Roger asked me to apologise for his absence, but he had to go to London on business and should be back later tonight.'

'Are he and Brett alike?'

'No, no, they're total opposites. The only thing they have in common is their passion for cars. Otherwise Roger takes after me and Brett's like his mother.' The old man sighed. 'Even after fifteen years I still miss her.'

'I didn't realise she'd died so long ago.'

'Brett was eighteen and Roger eight, though it affected Brett far more for he was deeply attached to her. For almost a year he wouldn't talk about her. He's a very emotional man, as I'm sure you know.'

Emma forbore to say she didn't, for Brett's father was showing her a side of his son she had never dreamed existed. She glanced across the room at him, and in that instant he looked up and met her gaze. He gave her a slow, sweet smile, and quickly she looked away, afraid he'd read her feelings in her face.

'I hope you'll look on this house as your home while you're here,' Mr Adams went on. 'If there's anything you need, just ask. You're Brett's wife, and one day you'll be mistress here. In fact as soon as he gives up racing and settles down, Roger and I will move to the lodge.'

'I hadn't realised this house would be Brett's,' Emma murmured. 'But why would you want to move out?'

'Because a married couple shouldn't have to live with their in-laws.'

'I don't think of you as an in-law. You're so much like Brett I feel completely relaxed with you.'

'Did you hear that?' Mr Adams called across to his son, obviously delighted, and when Brett shook his head, repeated what she had said.

'Emma always knows how to make people feel loved,' Brett answered, rising and moving across to them. 'That's one of the reasons I married her.'

'I don't need to ask the others,' his father smiled. 'They're apparent to anyone with eyes.'

'Talking about eyes,' Brett remarked, looking across at Emma, 'yours look as if they're ready to close! Why not have a rest? We won't be dining till eight-thirty, and I'll see that Cindy gets off to bed.'

'You must be tired too,' she replied.

'I wasn't flying the plane all night,' he said drily, and Emma gave a rueful laugh and took up his suggestion to have a rest.

It was seven-thirty when the alarm she had set awakened her, and she lay for a moment absorbing the stillness of the room. She had left the curtains undrawn, and moonlight streamed in through the two tall windows, silvering the outline of the dressing table and softening the edge of the two puffy armchairs that sat either side of the fireplace.

It was so still and quiet in here it was hard to believe there was an active household on the other side of the door, and with a contented little sigh she switched on the bedside lamp, bringing the room into colourful life again before padding into the bathroom for a luxurious soak.

She had just slipped on a fleecy towelling coat when she heard footsteps, and peering round the door saw Brett.

'Looking for something?' she asked, tightening the belt.

'That's a leading question,' he grinned. 'What are you offering?'

'Don't be silly. All I meant was why are you in my bedroom?'

'It's mine too.'

'I beg your pardon?'

'There's no need to apologise!' There was a glint in his eye. 'I've no objection to sharing it with you!'

'Well, I have.'

'I'm afraid you've no choice.' Brett was irritatingly calm. 'A load of relatives are arriving for Christmas, and as of tomorrow there won't be a spare room available. Besides, we're supposed to be happily married, and my father would be surprised if we didn't share a room.'

'He wouldn't be surprised if you told him the truth about us.'

'I'll do so in my own time.' Brett's voice had hardened and she recognised the obstinacy settling on his face.

'Why all the fuss at sharing a room with me?' he went on. 'What are you afraid of—me or yourself?'

'I'm certainly not afraid of myself.'

'Well you've no cause to be afraid of me, so you're making a scene for nothing. I told you before I'm not so hard up for a woman that I have to go where I'm not wanted.'

'I'm happy to hear it. But that still doesn't solve the problem.' She pointed to the four-poster. 'I might be willing to share a bedroom with you for a few days but I definitely won't share a bed.'

'We can adopt the old Norwegian custom and put a bolster down the middle.'

'For heaven's sake, be serious!' she said angrily.

'I am being serious. It's the way the villagers used to find out how strong-minded a man was. If the bolster was in the same position in the morning then——'

'Oh stop it!' she cried. 'I won't share a bed with you and that's final.'

Hearing the quiver in her voice, Brett sobered. 'I'm sorry about this, Emma, but short of putting up a camp bed in Roger's room there's not much I can do.'

'Then do it!'

'I'd rather not. It wouldn't take my relatives long to find out, and I don't relish having my private life chewed over.'

Emma looked at the bed and sighed heavily. 'It doesn't have a damned bolster!'

'We can put pillows down the middle.'

Brett was trying to maintain his serious expression

but clearly found it impossible, and seeing his mouth curve up at the corners, Emma couldn't help smiling too.

'I really am sorry,' he reiterated.

'It can't be helped. It was silly of me to get angry.'

He shrugged and loosened his tie. 'You're much more quick-tempered since we married,' he remarked.

This was all too true, but how could she tell him it was because she was trying to hide her love for him?

'It's probably nerves,' she excused herself. 'I'll try to do something about it.'

'Forget it. Once you've grown used to me you'll become your own sweet self again—lambasting me for doing all the wrong things with Cindy!'

Laughing, she sat at the dressing table and picked up her hair brush.

'Let me,' he said, and taking it from her began to brush her hair with rhythmical strokes.

Emma closed her eyes, enjoying the pleasure of his touch and the soothing movement of the brush. Only as it stopped did she open her eyes and meet his in the mirror.

'That was lovely,' she murmured.

'All part of the service,' he said laconically and, taking off his jacket, went over to the large walk-in cupboard to hang it up.

'I'll need to buy Cindy a complete winter wardrobe,' she said as he came out. 'And I'd like to go home and bring back my own.'

'Buy new.'

'That's what I thought you'd say! But it's such a waste of money when I've a stack of things mouldering away in cupboards.'

'It's only a waste of my money when you don't use it,' he declared. 'I'll take you into Harrogate tomorrow and you can go on a shopping spree.'

'Yes, boss.'

'I'm glad you recognise I am!'

With a toss of her head, she went into the cupboard and picked out a grey silk dress. Only then did she see all Brett's suits ranged along one wall and realised Millie must have done his unpacking.

Taking her dress into the bathroom, she put on fresh lingerie—one of the delicate satin sets Brett had bought her in Embira—then stepped into the dress. She was still buttoning it up as she came back into the room, and saw he was wearing a brocade silk dressing-gown, his bare legs below it clear indication that he was nude underneath.

'Grey,' he murmured, appraising her. 'You look like a nun.'

'Remember that!'

He laughed outright, the sound echoing in the room as he went to shower.

Reluctant to be in the bedroom when he came out, she picked up her handbag and went downstairs. The lights were on everywhere and the house had a golden glowing look which, together with the log fires merrily burning in the grates and the vases of gold and bronze chrysanthemums on several of the small tables, made her feel in the holiday spirit.

Her first Christmas as Brett's wife, yet should anything happen to him, it could also be the last!

'So you're my new sister-in-law,' an admiring voice said, and she swung round to see a gangling, fair-haired man on the threshold of the sitting-room. This was Roger, for the eyes were the colour of Brett's, though his skin was pale and his thick hair blond.

'Dad said you were pretty as a picture,' he went on, 'but I didn't realise he meant a Velázquez.'

'It's the grey dress,' she smiled, 'but don't let it fool you. Inside I'm all scarlet flounces!'

He chuckled and stepped back for her to enter the room, where his father was ensconced in a wing chair by the fire. Mr Adams looked older this evening, and Emma realised why Brett felt he wouldn't be a suitable guardian for a child of seven.

'This your first time in Yorkshire?' Roger asked, handing her a glass of champagne, and when she nodded, launched into a potted history of the moors.

'I forgot to tell you, Roger's a frustrated historian.' Brett sauntered into the room, cutting his brother short. 'With only minimal encouragement he'll take you through the centuries year by year!'

'We don't all think history began with the wheel!' Roger grinned, cuffing his brother's arm, and Brett poured himself a whisky and took a chair near his father.

In black pants and sweater, the top button open to reveal his throat, he looked saturnine and sensual, and as he glanced across his father's shoulder into Emma's eyes she had a feeling of power tightly leashed. Brett was in control of himself, but it would not take much for the control to break, and she knew she'd be well advised to tread carefully.

Later, seated at the dark oak table in the panelled dining-room, Emma almost had to pinch herself to believe she was here, sitting between two handsome men—one of whom was her husband—at a dinner hosted by a car magnate who was also her father-in-law! How little had she dreamed of this when Dr Walpole had advised her to accept the job in Brazil!

Stifling a sigh, she picked up her spoon and tackled the delicious vegetable soup, which was followed by rare roast beef and crunchy but moist Yorkshire pudding.

'Even if we're in the middle of a heat wave Mrs Ebson always serves this on my first night home,' Brett informed Emma.

'And very nice too,' she said, signalling her father-in-law that she couldn't eat more than one slice of meat.

'That's a portion for a bird,' he grumbled. 'No Yorkshire lass would be satisfied with that.'

'She's not a Yorkshire lass,' Brett grinned.

'She is now she's married to you, m'lad.'

'Well, maybe another very small slice,' Emma conceded, and was glad she had, for it was the tastiest she had eaten.

'I thought we'd decorate the Christmas tree tomorrow morning,' Mr Adams announced.

'Emma and I are going shopping in Harrogate,' Brett said. 'Neither of my women have any winter clothes!'

'They're forecasting snow,' Roger announced. 'With any luck we'll have a white Christmas.'

'With impassable roads and half the men not turning up for work,' Mr Adams grumbled.

This turned the talk to business and, unable to contribute to the conversation, Emma let her mind drift. She felt very much at home in the lovely house, even though she had only been there a few hours, and didn't understand how Brett could bear to leave it. The villa in Mertola was lovely and the weather perfect there, but this stone manor epitomised all that was best of England.

'Tired?' Brett's voice, soft in her ear, made her realise her eyes had half closed.

'A little,' she said.

'Try and eat a bit more. You've hardly touched a thing.'

'I know, but it was a big portion.'

'Some fruit, then?'

He reached out to the silver bowl on the centre of the table and carefully selected a luscious-looking peach, which he placed on Emma's plate.

She began to peel off the velvety skin and, conscious of three pairs of eyes on her, found that her fingers trembled. Brett leaned over, and taking the peach and knife from her finished the job. He cut the fruit precisely into segments and returned the plate to her. As Emma began to eat she noticed an odd expression flit across her father-in-law's face.

'Thinking of giving up racing yet?' Roger suddenly asked his brother.

Emma kept her eyes lowered and pretended not to be listening, though she was keenly aware of Brett looking in her direction as he answered. 'What I do depends on Emma.'

Startled, she looked up at this, directly into whimsical eyes whose expression she could not analyse.

'How do you feel about it, Emma?' Mr Adams questioned.

'Naturally I'd like him to stop racing,' she said slowly. 'But don't let him kid you it's my decision. Brett's his own man and will do as he wishes. That's something I accepted when I married him.'

'Clever girl,' Mr Adams acknowledged. 'The best way of getting anyone to do as you want is not to ask them.'

'I wish *you*'d remember that, Dad,' Roger chipped in, and his father chuckled.

'Trouble is, it's easier to give advice than take it,' he admitted. 'But now Brett's got a wife, I'll leave him to her.'

Crumpling his napkin he led the way into the sitting-room, where the conversation continued to focus on cars. Claiming tiredness, Emma went to her room. Her room and Brett's, she reminded herself, and glancing at the four-poster, saw two pillows lying like a bolster down the middle of it.

'Fat lot of use they'd be if Brett took it into his head to . . .'

In a fit of exasperation she grabbed them up and flung them on to a chair. She was damned if she'd give him the satisfaction of knowing how scared she was. She'd play it cool if it killed her!

Trouble was, she was worried sick, not because of what Brett might do but because of how she might respond to it. If only she didn't love him so much. But she did, and earlier this evening she had realised how difficult it was going to be to resist him if he made a move towards her. She had wandered into the library and seen a pile of racing magazines which she had glanced through. Every one of them had contained pictures of Brett. Some were action shots on the race track but most showed him beside his car, invariably with a beautiful girl hanging on his arm.

What need had he of inexperienced little Emma, when he had an open invitation from some of the loveliest women in café society? Still, lovely or not, he hadn't considered marrying one of them, and she hugged this knowledge close as she undressed and opened a drawer to find a nightgown.

To her dismay she realised they were all flimsy, and though she put on the least revealing one, it did little to hide her pointed breasts and the gentle curve of her thighs.

Nervously she slipped between the lavender-scented sheets. An electric blanket had been switched on, and she found it uncomfortably warm. Quickly she turned it off. Men didn't like heat anyway, and it would be less dangerous for Brett's libido for him to lie on a cool mattress. Pity she couldn't put ice in the springs!

A chuckle escaped her, but it was surface humour only and almost at once she was anxious again. She longed to be asleep when he came in but had never felt more wide awake in her life. Still, if she went on sitting up, she'd never sleep, and she curled herself beneath the duvet and closed her eyes.

Gradually her eyelids grew heavy, her limbs seemed to float and she lost consciousness.

The creak of the bedroom door brought Emma instantly

awake. Heart pounding in her throat, she forced herself
to lie still and keep her eyes closed.

Footsteps came softly across the carpet and stopped
at the side of the bed. She tensed as she felt Brett bend
down, and heard him emit a faint sigh as he straightened
and moved away. Still not daring to open her eyes, she
tried to gauge what he was doing. A drawer creaked, a
cupboard opened and she guessed he was undressing.

A shaft of light cutting across the carpet told her he
was going into the bathroom, and only as the room
darkened again did she sit up and draw a deep breath.
She heard a tap running and the clink of a glass, then
the light seeping from under the door vanished, and
she quickly lay down again and turned her face into the
pillow.

The mattress of the four-poster sank slightly beneath
Brett's weight as he slipped into bed, and she was
suddenly struck by the ludicrousness of the situation.
Here she was, lying next to the man she loved, yet
curled so far away from him that one wrong movement
would send her crashing to the floor. A bubble of
laughter escaped her and hearing it, Brett leaned
towards her.

'So you're awake?' he said in a satisfied tone. 'I
knew it.'

'How?'

'Your eyelids were moving.'

'Rapid eye movements,' she retorted. 'Dreaming.'

'Rapid eye movements, my foot! You looked like a
scared rabbit.'

He moved again, and she sensed he was leaning up
on one elbow. 'By the way, where's the makeshift
bolster?'

'I got rid of it. I'm not afraid of you.'

'Commendable but foolish,' he commented. 'I'm
afraid of myself!'

Emma's cheeks burned, and she was glad the room

was lit only by moonlight, for though it revealed their outlines he could not see the scarlet of her face.

'I've been married to you for five celibate weeks,' he went on softly. 'You should have thought of that before getting rid of the pillows.'

'I'm n-not f-frightened of you,' she reiterated tremulously.

'I hope you feel more confident than you sound!'

'I have every confidence in myself. Anyway, you had no need to be celibate. I didn't ask you to give up other women.'

Brett was so long replying, Emma was sorry her tongue had run away with her. Some things were best left unsaid, and that was definitely the case where Brett's sexual life was concerned.

'You may have given me my sexual freedom with one hand, but you took it away with the other,' he said whimsically.

'What do you mean?'

'Well, I could hardly have gone with another woman in Mertola or Embira without it becoming common knowledge! And as you insisted I be circumspect, I had no choice but to be celibate!'

'I see.' She moistened lips that were uncomfortably dry. 'Well, you shouldn't have that difficulty in England. I'm sure you often go to London.'

'True,' he said equably. 'But I'll have to take cold baths until after Christmas, because I've no hope of getting away till the New Year.' He thumped his pillow and lay back on it. 'Frustrated I may be, Emma, but I'm not so far gone that you need perch on the edge of the bed like a demented hen! I'm tired and jet-lagged and I intend having a good night's sleep.'

Deliberately he moved closer to the centre of the bed. 'You rather spoil my pleasure you know,' he added. 'Having a wife who'll accept my playing around takes the edge off my desire to do so!'

'I'm sure it won't stop you, though.'

'It won't, don't worry.'

'Good.' She turned her back on him, almost jumping out of her skin as his hand touched her shoulder.

'For God's sake!' he groaned. 'I only wanted to say I'm sorry.'

'For what?'

'For my sarcasm. You've obviously never shared a bed with a man. Never shared anything with a man, in fact, and having me here can't be easy for you.'

It wasn't, though not for the reasons he thought, and Emma wondered what he'd do if she turned and flung herself into his arms. Make love to her properly, no doubt. But no, he wouldn't. He'd only make sex! She sighed, and he heard the sound and gave her shoulder another reassuring squeeze.

'Let's not have a quarrel between us on our first night here,' he said.

'Perhaps a pillow would have been preferable!' she mumbled.

His chuckle stayed with her long after he had fallen asleep, and listening to his quiet breathing she fought the urge to inch closer to the warmth of him. Five weeks of celibacy, eh? Though he had said it was because he wished to avoid gossip, she didn't believe him. He could easily have gone to Rio for a weekend, but had made no move to do so. She was still wondering why when she eventually fell asleep.

She awoke to a room flooded with daylight, and to the awareness of lying enclosed in Brett's arms. Only total exhaustion from her flight home could have made it possible for her to sleep so soundly in this intimate position.

Cautiously she tried to move, anxious to escape his hold before he awoke. But her hope of doing so was dashed when he tightened his grip and said thickly,

'For God's sake, lie still. You've been in my arms half the night, so what's a few more minutes?'

'Half the night?' she croaked. 'You're joking!'

'Scout's honour.'

Emma attempted to turn her head, but his cheek was on her hair and she lay still again, her body starting to tingle with desire. This was ridiculous. She must escape before she gave herself away.

'I'm sorry I spoiled your night,' she muttered. 'You should have pushed me away.'

'I tried, but you kept moving back!'

'I must have been in a pretty deep sleep,' she said crossly.

'Are you suggesting I inveigled you into my arms?'

'Even *you* couldn't do that!'

A chuckle rumbled through his chest, and as his hold on her loosened, she leapt out of bed and reached for her dressing-gown.

'Call me old-fashioned if you like, but I really can't share a bed with you again, Brett. Tell your father I'm claustrophobic.'

'That's from being in a confined space, not a confined bed!'

'You know what I mean.'

'Only too well,' he grinned.

It was impossible for her not to smile, though she had no intention of backing down on what she had said.

'I mean it, Brett. I won't share a bed with you again, so stop treating the whole thing as a joke.'

Before he could reply, she ran into the bathroom and banged the door shut. As she soaked in a hot bath her temper cooled, and she was ashamed of the scene she had made. Still, she hadn't given away the real reason for her anger, which had come from the knowledge that Brett had held her half the night yet hadn't made love to her. So much for her belief that he desired her even though he didn't love her!

Tears coursed down her face and she splashed cold water on it before drying herself and returning to the bedroom. Brett was sitting up against the pillows calmly drinking a cup of coffee and glancing at the morning paper.

He took no notice of her and she looked at him out of the corner of her eye as she collected fresh lingerie from a drawer. He was wearing pale blue silk pyjamas, the jacket fitting so snugly across his chest that she was sure it belonged to Roger. She was also sure Brett slept nude, and wondered humorously what excuse he had made to his brother when he had asked to borrow a pair of pyjamas! Thank heavens he had. She would really have had a fit if he'd shared her bed wearing nothing.

'Yours is in there.' He nodded towards the coffee-pot standing on a tray beside the bed.

'Coffee doesn't agree with me first thing in the morning,' she said, gathering up slacks and a sweater— the warmest things she had—and taking them into the bathroom.

'If I'd known how strongly you felt about sharing a room with me,' he announced as she came out of the bathroom wearing them, 'I'd have dossed down in the study last night. But I never expected you to behave like a frightened virgin.'

'I may be a virgin,' she snapped, 'but I'm not frightened! I simply don't want——'

'I'm not interested in your wants,' he cut across her, 'any more than you're interested in mine. I'm only surprised that someone who's so warm with children can be so unfeeling towards an adult.'

'Just because I don't feel anything for *you* doesn't mean I'm unfeeling!'

Silence met her remark, and as she went to the

dressing-table, she saw him staring down at the morning paper.

'How do you feel about staying here with Cindy for a few months?' he asked abruptly.

She swivelled round on the stool. 'I thought we were going to travel with you?'

'I've changed my mind. It's better if the two of you stay in England.'

She turned back to the mirror. 'Anything you say, Brett.'

'That's settled then. My father will be delighted.' Brett poured himself another coffee. 'In fact you might as well enrol Cindy in the local school.'

'I thought we agreed I'd teach her for the next few years?'

'Only if you'd been travelling with me. But if you live here . . .'

'Very well.' Emma smoothed her hair. 'With Cindy at day school and you away, I'm going to feel redundant.'

'I'm sure you can find a worthy cause in which to involve yourself.'

'I wish I'd never married you!' she burst out.

'What's brought this on?'

'Don't pretend you don't know!' Emma cried. 'Cindy feels completely at home with your father and Roger, and now she's secure in your love too, there's no need for me to be around.'

'You're talking nonsense. Sure Cindy loves my family, but she still needs a woman to turn to—and you're the best.'

He set down his cup and stretched his arms above his head. A button on his pyjama jacket popped and she saw a wide expanse of bronzed, satiny skin. Getting up, she retrieved the button from the carpet and held it out to him.

'Your jacket's too small,' she said expressionlessly.

'I'm bigger than Roger.'

So she had been right. 'Would you like me to sew it on for you?'

'That's a very wifely thing to do.'

'There are certain aspects of the role I'm prepared to play.'

'You should type them out some time and let me have it. Then I'll know what demands to make.'

Trembling with rage, Emma returned to the dressing table and rummaged in her jewel box for a pair of earrings. Hiding her feelings for Brett wasn't doing her temper any good, and sooner or later it would lead to a bitter quarrel which would result in their parting. Because of Cindy she was loath for this to happen, and knew the only way to prevent it was to distance herself from Brett.

Hands casual in the pockets of her slacks, she paused by the door. 'You're right in suggesting Cindy and I stay here. And if I'm bored I'll look around for part-time work.'

'I knew you'd see it my way.' He glanced up from the paper, his eyes curiously blank. 'That's what I like about you, Emma. You're always so logical.'

If only he knew how wrong he was, how much she wanted to discard logic and fling herself into his arms! Instead she closed the door behind her and went downstairs to breakfast.

CHAPTER ELEVEN

EMMA was not surprised when Brett excused himself from going with her and Cindy to Harrogate, pleading an unexpected business appointment. However, he arranged for the chauffeur to drive them, and they spent the best part of the day shopping.

Hurt by her quarrel with him, she flung economy to the winds and chose a winter wardrobe without any concession to price. Brett might not find her as fanciable as he did his numerous girlfriends, but she was hell bent on showing him that even virginal governesses could look stunning if they wished.

Her earlier fear that if he found her attractive he'd try to seduce her no longer existed, for any full-blooded man who could hold a near-naked young woman in his arms—and one who was not only attractive but his wife to boot—must be so determined to keep his marriage platonic that she could share his bed for ever without putting herself at risk!

By the time she and Cindy returned home, it was snowing. A white dusting covered the driveway, and glittering flakes lay like petals on the roof of the house and the surrounding trees and bushes. It was a traditional Christmas scene and Emma felt tears sting her eyes. How perfect this would be if only Brett loved her.

'May I put on my party dress tonight?' Cindy asked excitedly as Ebson opened the door to them.

'I thought you'd wear it for Christmas Day,' Emma

said. 'But there's no reason why you can't unpack everything we bought and put them away.'

'If you say so, Emma,' Cindy said in unconscious imitation of her father—it being a phrase he'd frequently used of late—and danced off upstairs, Ebson following more slowly, laden with boxes.

Smilingly Emma watched her. What a happy transformation there'd been in Cindy since she'd first met her: from imperious, fantasy-ridden rebel to joyous, amenable child.

Behind her, Emma heard the sitting-room door open, and turned to see her father-in-law there.

'Had a successful day?' he asked.

'An expensive one,' she said wryly. 'Brett will have a shock when he sees the bills.'

'But not when he sees you and Cindy in the clothes! Now come and sit by the fire and have some tea.'

Touched by his solicitude, she did as he suggested.

'Is Brett still at the factory?' she asked, accepting a buttered crumpet and biting into it.

'No. He only stayed an hour, then said he felt restless and went for a walk on the moor. Came back half-frozen too.' Mr Adams frowned. 'He'd have done better to have gone with you to Harrogate.'

'That would have made him even more restless!'

'I don't think so. I think you're the only one who can calm him. He cares for you very deeply, you know.'

Emma kept her face averted. Let Mr Adams have his illusions. He obviously wanted to believe his elder son was happy, and would realise soon enough that this wasn't true.

'I never thought he'd marry again after Eileen,' Mr Adams continued. 'She gave him such hell that I feared it would put him off marriage for life.'

Unable to see it this way—Eileen seemed more wronged against than wrong—Emma held her tongue.

'I'm assuming Brett's told you about it?' Mr Adams questioned. 'Your silence makes me wonder.'

'He—er—he hasn't,' Emma stumbled. 'The little I know came from Diana.'

Mr Adams looked disgusted. 'All she'll do is repeat her parents' version—and they were as dishonest as Eileen!'

'Dishonest?'

'Absolutely. It's my belief—always has been—that they were in on the deception from the start.'

Emma had no idea what her father-in-law was talking about, and reading it on her face, Mr Adams snorted again.

'It would seem my son's carried gentlemanly silence too far. If anyone's entitled to know the full story it's you.'

'Maybe Brett doesn't want me to know,' Emma said quickly, 'and if that's how he feels then perhaps I——'

'Twaddle!' Mr Adam's silver thatch of hair glinted in the firelight as he leaned forward. 'You knew Eileen was older than Brett, of course?'

'No I didn't.'

'Well she was—by nine years.'

Emma was surprised. 'She didn't look it in the photograph I saw. I thought her young and very beautiful.'

'Unfortunately her looks were no indication of her character, though Brett didn't realise it until too late. He was twenty-two when they met and she bowled him over completely.' Mr Adams picked up a pair of brass tongs and poked vigorously at the logs. Sparks flew from them like erupting anger. 'She deliberately seduced him, you know. Set her cap at him and wouldn't leave him alone. I warned him not to get engaged but he was too besotted over her to listen to me, and by the time he came to his senses it was too late. She told him she was expecting his baby and threatened to kill herself if he didn't marry her. I pleaded with him to call her bluff but he refused. Said he felt morally obliged to go through with it.'

'If he hadn't and anything had happened to her, the publicity would have ruined him.'

'Did Diana tell you that too?'

'Yes.'

'There's not a word of truth in it. Brett was only beginning to make his name at that time, and certainly wouldn't have merited the attention of the press. No, he married Eileen for the reason he gave me—obligation—and a few months later discovered he'd been played for a fool.'

'What do you mean?'

Mr Adam's hands trembled with remembered indignation. 'The pregnancy turned out to be pure fabrication.'

'But Cindy was——'

'Born a few years later. Not because Eileen wanted her—she didn't have an ounce of maternal love in her—but because she thought having Brett's child would make him stay with her.'

Emma tried to take in this new version of Brett's marriage, but common sense warned her that Mr Adams's account of it could be as biased in his son's favour as Diana's was biased in her sister's.

'If Brett was unhappy with Eileen, why didn't he leave her when he found out she wasn't pregnant?'

'Because he was too kind-hearted. He tried to leave her twice in the first year but each time she took an overdose. Then Cindy was born and Brett made every effort to save the marriage. But it was a losing battle. Eileen was mentally unstable—paranoid jealousy—something her parents knew, though they'd managed to keep it hidden. As a youngster she'd tried to kill Diana because she thought they loved her sister more than herself. You see, if she loved you, she had to possess you a hundred per cent of the time, had to know what you were doing, thinking, saying.'

'Brett must have felt as if he were in prison!'

'With a sentence that would never end. Racing was his only escape. In the beginning he'd done it as a hobby, and to help get our cars known. But as his marriage grew worse, he turned to it more and more. Took incredible chances on the track too. Almost as if he had a death wish. And of course that made Eileen worse.'

'Understandable.' Emma was on home ground here. 'If you love someone you don't enjoy knowing they're risking their neck for nothing.'

'I think there were times when my son thought death preferable to living with his wife,' Mr Adams sighed. 'In fact at one stage I considered pulling out of racing. Except that if I had, Brett would have gone to another firm. And then, almost like a miracle—Eileen changed. It was one Christmas when they were here. I saw it for myself and couldn't believe it. She stopped acting possessively, didn't make a scene if Brett talked to another woman, and eventually went off for a jaunt round Europe with another man—just to show Brett she wasn't going to tie him down!'

'A somewhat dramatic way of making a point,' Emma exclaimed.

'That was Eileen all over, doing things to extremes, and not realising she'd given Brett the opportunity he'd been waiting for. He wrote and told her he was happy she'd found someone else, and that he was filing for divorce. Eileen came dashing back saying she'd only been trying to show him she wasn't possessive any longer, and begging him to give her another chance. But Brett had had enough. He said it was best for both of them if they were free, and returned to Brazil with Cindy—Eileen had left the child when she'd gone off round Europe. Well, naturally Eileen wasn't going to give him up so easily. She bombarded him with phone calls and letters, she actually slashed her wrists in her doctor's waiting-room—to make sure she'd be saved, I always said—and Brett finally caved in and agreed to take her back. She was on her way to Mertola when she was killed in a plane crash.'

For several moments Emma absorbed what she had heard. This was not the same story re-coloured by another person's point of view, but a different story entirely, and she had to make up her mind which one to believe.

'Are you saying Eileen wasn't running away from Brett when she was killed?'

'Why should you think otherwise? Even the Proctors couldn't lie about that!'

'I'm afraid Diana did.'

Mr Adams muttered angrily beneath his breath, then shook his head. 'I dare say Brett played into the Proctors' hands by the way he acted after she was killed. He kept blaming himself for it, said he should have been more understanding of her and tried to help her. But believe me, there was nothing he could have done. She'd never faced the truth about her illness, wouldn't even admit there was anything wrong with her.'

The old man edged his chair nearer the fire, as if talking of unhappy events had made him cold. 'I hoped her death would enable him to live a normal life. But it did the opposite. He no longer trusted women and refused to take them seriously. It was one affair after the other, and if any of them showed any sign of caring for him, he ran a mile. I never thought I'd live to see the day he married again. Which just shows what love can do! Brett said he took one look at you and was a free man again.'

'Free?' Emma was puzzled.

'That's what he said. "Free to love a woman without being afraid she'll try to destroy my identity."'

Emma gazed down at her lap. What a clever liar Brett was! She appreciated his desire to reassure his father, but wished he hadn't pretended to be quite so crazy about her.

'He called you a firebrand who'd made him face up to the truth,' Mr Adams went on amusedly. '"I listened to Emma and I found myself, then I took another look at her and lost myself again!"'

This was too much for Emma to bear and she jumped to her feet.

'It's not true, Mr Adams. I really can't . . . I don't want to be a party to any more lies.'

'Lies?' Mr Adams was startled. 'I don't know what you mean.'

'I mean that Brett was lying. He doesn't love me. He never has. He married me so I'd be Cindy's legal guardian if anything happened to him. He's so worried the Proctors could——'

Mr Adam's rumbling laugh drowned the rest of Emma's words.

'You're quite wrong, my dear,' he said when he could speak again. 'Cindy would have had a loving home with my niece, Mary. She's married and has three sons of her own, and would like nothing better than a daughter. She and Brett practically grew up together. You'll meet her and her family here tomorrow.'

'Then why did he marry me?' Emma was bewildered.

'For the same reason you married him, I dare say.

And don't expect me to believe you only did it to give Cindy a home. I may be old but I'm not senile!'

Emma swallowed convulsively. It was embarrassing to reveal her inner feelings, but she liked Mr Adams too much to lie to him.

'Am I so transparent?' she asked shakily.

'To me you are. But then my years have given me the ability—not always welcome, I can assure you— to see the wood for the trees. I know you love Brett. It's in your eyes when you look at him—and in his when he looks at you! I watched him peel that peach for you last night, and I've never seen him so caring or tender towards anyone. He didn't realise how much of his feelings he was giving away.'

'By peeling a peach!'

'By the expression on his face as he looked at you. Surely you aren't blind to it?'

'Let's say I'm so scared of reading more into it than is there, that I won't let myself see anything.'

'Then take my word for it. I wouldn't lie to you, Emma; there'd be no point. My son loves you. I'm sure of it.'

It was all Emma could do not to rush out to find Brett. Yet she held back, scared that her father-in-law had said what he wanted to believe rather than what was true. On the other hand he could be right, and if he were, what did she intend doing about it?

'I think I'll go find Cindy,' she murmured. 'Thanks for the tea and—and everything you said.'

'Will you act on it?'

'I'm not sure.'

'You'll be making a mistake if you don't.'

With these words ringing in her ears, Emma went in search of Cindy.

CHAPTER TWELVE

A SEARCH of the house finally brought Emma to the kitchen, where Cindy was helping Mrs Ebson make mince pies. She was so engrossed with putting in the filling and covering them with their pastry tops that she was unaware of being watched.

What a lovely child she was. Emma dreaded to think what would have happened to Cindy if she hadn't gone to Brazil as her governess, and thanked the benevolent fates that had made her accept the job. Little had she known when she did that it would change her own life as much as the child's, bringing her the joy of being near Brett as well as the fear that it could not last.

Yet if her father-in-law was right . . . But he couldn't be!

On the other hand, how could she be positive without actually asking Brett? The thought of his astonishment if she did—and the amused denial he'd make—made her writhe with shame and put the idea of questioning him from her mind.

But it returned more forcibly, bringing other questions with it. Was she so full of pride that she was unwilling to risk a rebuff from Brett? And even if he didn't love her, maybe he was beginning to care for her, a caring that he might admit if she disclosed her own feelings.

Cindy glanced up and waved a floury hand, grinning from ear to ear. The sight made Emma's heart overflow with love, and knowing how wonderful it would be for Cindy to have parents who loved each other, she knew she had to talk to Brett regardless.

'Have you seen Daddy?' she asked.

'I think he's gone to look at one of the cars in the garage.'

Grabbing an anorak from a pile hanging in the back lobby, Emma went out. The snow was coming down thickly and the sky was growing dark with approaching night. She trudged towards the garages, more nervous with every step. If Brett cared for her, why had he changed his mind about letting her and Cindy travel with him? Did he dislike her too much to be bothered with her, or love her too much to trust himself to be with her? Either way she had to find out, for their relationship could not continue as it was, not now she knew about his cousin who made her own presence in Cindy's life superfluous.

Knowing that if Brett proved his father wrong she could find herself back at the nursery school, Emma approached the garage with a heavy heart. She heard voices, but entering, found only the chauffeur, and a middle-aged man emerging from a BMW.

'You're Brett's wife,' he said instantly, coming towards her with outstretched hand. 'I'm Marcus Longbridge, Brett's uncle by marriage.'

Emma returned with him to the house, answering his questions about Cindy and Brett, though afterwards she was totally unable to recall what she had said.

'Come into the library and meet the rest of my family,' he said jovially, handing his overcoat to Ebson.

The prospect of making small talk with people she didn't know—or even with those she did—was more than she could face at this moment, and murmuring that she had to go to her room first, she ran upstairs.

She was a few yards from her bedroom when the door opened and Brett came out. Seeing her eye the pyjamas and dressing-gown draped over his arm, he said mockingly, 'I've put up a camp bed in Roger's room.'

'I thought you were reluctant to do that?'

'Needs must when the devil drives,' he shrugged. 'Not that you're the devil,' he added hastily. 'But as it obviously upsets you to share a room with me——'

'We've got to talk,' Emma interrupted, and pushed past him.

'What about?' he asked, following her into the bedroom and closing the door.

'About us, and why you didn't tell me that your cousin would look after Cindy if anything happened to you.'

'Oh, that,' he drawled, leaning against the door. 'Who's been talking to you?'

'Your father.'

Brett pulled a face, signifying his realisation that it was pointless to deny it.

'Why did you get me to marry you under false pretences?' Emma demanded.

'Does it matter?'

'Of course it matters! I'd never have agreed if I'd known the truth.'

'That's why I didn't tell you! You see I thought—I still think—Cindy will be happier with you than anyone else. I love Mary dearly, but she had three rumbustious boys and Cindy would have to vie with them for attention. Whereas with you, she'd get it without asking.'

It was a valid reason, and Emma's own reasoning faltered at it.

'Well?' Brett said, 'Satisfied?'

'I think so.' But she wasn't, and would regret it for ever if cowardice kept her silent. 'Was it only because of Cindy that you married me?'

Although he remained leaning nonchalantly against the door, she sensed a wariness about him.

'You shouldn't listen to my father, Emma. He's given to romantic notions.'

'Like suggesting you married me because you love me?'

'My God!' A nerve twitched at the side of Brett's mouth. 'Is that what he said?'

'Among other things.' She was trembling so much she could barely stand. 'Was he wrong, Brett?'

'Wrong?'

'Don't prevaricate! Be honest with me for once in your life. I can't play these sort of games with you, Brett. You're a worldly man and you can run rings around me.'

'That's odd,' he said jerkily. 'I'd say that's exactly what you do to me! One glance from these lovely eyes of yours and I don't know whether I'm coming or going.' With a gesture of fury he flung his pyjamas to the floor. 'Don't you know what you do to me, for God's sake?'

'If I did I wouldn't be asking you! Did you or did you not marry me because of Cindy?'

'No, dammit, no! It was for me—because I needed you! I love you' he said thickly. 'I don't know when I first realised it but I—I—suddenly knew I couldn't let you walk out of my life. When I saw how fond you were of Cindy, I——'

Emma gave him no chance to finish, for with a cry of joy she flung herself into his arms.

'I love you too!' she cried over and over again. 'Couldn't you see it? Couldn't you tell?'

For answer he grabbed her close, his arms bands of steel, his eyes glowing gold as joy lit them.

'You love me? Do you know what you're saying?'

'Only too well. I've loved you for months, Brett, and been frightened out of my wits that you'd guess.

I'd have gone on hiding it if your father hadn't made me see how impossible it was.'

'Impossible for me too,' Brett groaned, pressing his lips against the side of her throat. 'If you knew the torment I was in last night holding you in my arms and wanting you so much I nearly went crazy. I still can't believe you love me,' he said, and swinging her up into his arms, carried her to the bed.

As Emma sank on to the mattress she held up her arms to him, and he came down beside her, pressing his body against hers.

'I need you so much,' he whispered into her hair. 'I swore I'd never let another woman come close to me again, but you wormed your way into my heart before I knew it.'

'Then why did you say Cindy and I shouldn't travel with you?' she asked.

'Because I was dead scared I'd give myself away.'

Tears glittered on her lashes and he licked at them. 'What a time to cry!'

'I always cry when I'm happy.'

'Then I'd better buy shares in Kleenex, because I aim to make you happy for the rest of your life! You've bewitched me, Emma mine. Love's trussed me like a chicken and I'm loving it. I couldn't bear it when you kept saying I could do as I liked and you'd go along with all my decisions. I longed for our marriage to be a partnership, a sharing of everything.' Moving slightly away from her, he looked into her eyes. 'Will you travel around the world with me, Emma?'

'Don't you know my middle name's Ruth? "Whither thou goest, I will go."'

The smile that played about his mouth moved to his eyes. 'I won't put you through it, my darling.'

'Put me through it?'

'Having you live in constant fear for my safety. I

know now what Eileen went through, though I didn't realise it until I fell in love with *you*.' Anguish marked his face as he sat up straight. 'You see, I never loved Eileen, so I couldn't understand what she went through. I was an arrogant swine, Emma, and I must have made her life hell.'

'No more of a hell than she made yours,' Emma said firmly, determined not to let him flay himself needlessly. There was a great deal more to be said but she knew now was not the time. Later they would talk candidly about his marriage.

'You always know when you've said enough,' Brett murmured, bending over her.

'I'll remind you of that the day you tell me I'm nagging you!'

He chuckled, and Emma touched her fingers to his curving mouth and marvelled that she could do so without embarrassment. This was Brett, the man she loved, though not yet her lover, and she would have no secrets from him, hide none of her emotions.

'Don't ever leave me behind when you go away,' she whispered. 'I can't bear to be parted from you.'

'Nor me, you. But I've no plans to go away, sweetheart. My racing days are over. That's what I've been trying to tell you.'

She stared at him in wonderment.

'I mean it,' he reiterated. 'I don't want to risk my life any more. I've too much to live for.'

'Will you be happy without racing?' Emma asked. 'Some men need that sort of excitement and——'

'Not me. If I'd been happy with Eileen I'd have given it up years ago. Then when she died I felt too guilty to pull out. I believed my racing had killed her and the only way I could expiate my guilt was to carry on with it.'

Though he spoke matter-of-factly, Emma guessed at the agony of remorse that had made him live his life so dangerously for so long, and thanked God he no longer felt the need to do so. Yet when she spoke she was deliberately casual.

'You'll never be a stay-at-home husband,' she teased.

'Not on a regular basis,' he admitted. 'While Dad's in charge, I intend being sales manager—which means travelling the world for several months each year. Both of us,' he warned.

Lifting her hands, he kissed each finger, then moved his mouth along her arm and up the side of her throat. As he reached her lips his kisses became fiercer, the flame of desire burning between them.

Eagerly they undressed each other, fragile silk tearing, buttons flying in their need to come together, though Brett was in sufficient control to stride to the door and lock it before pulling her into his arms to make her his own.

Avidly they drank of one another, their tongues exploring with unashamed bliss. Brett kissed her breasts, sucking the nipples till they stood erect like twin beacons of love, and all the while his hands caressed her, stroking her skin and searching out the intimate recesses of her thighs and what lay between.

Surging with love for him, Emma experienced a frenzy of delight as the soft hairs on his chest prickled her face. His swelling manhood pressed into her side and as he touched her more and more intimately, she felt herself grow tumescent. No barrier—emotional or physical—separated them. The misery of the past weeks was over and they could luxuriate in their knowledge of each other. With a soft cry she arched her body beneath his, and he responded by mounting her.

Lifting her legs wide to receive him, she gave a cry of ecstasy as he plunged into her, thrusting deep and fierce until her cries became gasps and her pelvic muscles contracted around him.

He groaned deep in his throat, the sound one of pure joy as her contractions acted like supple fingers on the essence of his being. His movements grew faster and she felt him swell inside her, growing so large that there was no part of her he did not fill.

In an ecstasy of desire she pressed closer, lifting her legs higher so that she lay open to him like a flower, the inner core of her femininity throbbing with passion as he stroked it with his fingers, all the while continuing to plunge into her until, with a cry, he flooded her with the liquid of his love.

'Brett, Brett,' she moaned, and her shuddering climax joined his.

For a long while they lay together, his arms wrapping her against the world, though beyond the bedroom door they heard laughter and voices that told them they could not keep it at bay too long. There was the sound of a car in the drive, doors being slammed, and the excited bark of a dog.

'That's Mary and Jack with their boys,' Brett said against Emma's ear. 'She's bringing Cindy a puppy.'

'What a wonderful present!' Emma tilted her head to look into his face. 'I longed to buy you something special, Brett, but I was so afraid of giving myself away that I chose the safest gift I could—gold cufflinks!'

'I had the same problem with you,' came his amused reply. 'So all you're getting is a gold necklace!'

'And *you*!' She wrapped her arms around him. 'You're the best present for me. Just you.'

'Echoed in triplicate!' He kissed the tip of her nose. 'Know something, Emma? I think I'm catching a cold.'

'Oh, darling, no!'

'Oh, darling, yes. Looks as if I'll have to stay in bed for Christmas.'

It took only an instant for Emma to follow his train of thought, and she hit him hard. 'You wouldn't dare!'

'Wouldn't I?'

Drawing aside the sheet, he disclosed the swelling sign of his passion. 'I want to be inside you the whole time, Emma, filling you with me again and again until you cry out for mercy.'

She gave a cry now and pulled him on top of her, spreading her legs to give him instant access.

'Don't wait,' she whispered. 'Quickly, Brett. I want you so much. *Oh . . .*'

Her voice spiralled higher and higher, as he penetrated to the very heart of her. She experienced the greatest intensity of love for him, and knew with intuitive clarity that their life forces had met to create a physical manifestation of their union. Her hands fluttered over his face as he gasped and rolled on to his side, drawing her close to his heart.

At last, still languorous with love, she stretched like a kitten and yawned. 'Time to get up, Brett.'

'No pretended cold?'

'Regrettably not.'

'But early nights, though?'

'Very early nights.'

He reached for her again, but lithely avoiding his hands, she slipped from the bed and padded into the bathroom to run the shower, turning the key in the lock with a triumphant laugh even as Brett tried to come in.

'That's a very unsociable thing to do,' he called.

'But necessary,' she giggled. 'If you come in we'll never get downstairs in time for dinner.'

His answering laugh told her she was right, and smiling, she soaked herself, enjoying the sensuous feel of the water on her skin. She felt tinglingly alive, her breasts still heavy with love, her muscles aching from the fierce hold of her husband.

Her husband. She repeated the words, enjoying the pleasure they gave her, and repeating them some half-hour later as she and Brett left the bedroom hand in hand and walked along the corridor: a tall broad-shouldered, mahogany-haired man; a graceful toffee-blonde who reached as high as his heart.

At the first stair they stopped. All Brett's relations were in the hall, and as they slowly went down to greet them, Emma met her father-in-law's eyes.

'All well?' he called softly, his lined face creasing into a smile.

'Very well,' Brett and Emma answered in unison, then looked at each other and laughed happily before going forward to greet the family.

Take 4 novels and a surprise gift FREE

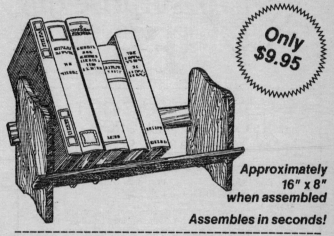

Harlequin Presents

Coming Next Month

1031 WINTER SUNLIGHT Susan Alexander
Sophie can't believe it. Max is offering her what she most wants. But marriage with Max, an eminent Austrian baron, is not for her. She can love him, have an affair with him. But not marriage!

1032 NIGHT OF THE CONDOR Sara Craven
Crossing the world to join her fiancé in Peru changes spoiled wealthy Leigh Frazier's life. For in meeting the fascinating archeologist Dr. Rourke Martinez, she is drawn under the spell of the high Andes, in a new and dangerous embrace....

1033 THE ONE THAT GOT AWAY Emma Darcy
Substituting as skipper on her father's fishing boat, chartered by American football player and movie star, Taylor Marshall, Jillian realizes after she falls in love, that to him it's just another game. And will she be just another trophy?

1034 SINGLE COMBAT Sandra Field
Lydia grew up without love. She's learned to live without it, she thinks. Now here's James who simply refuses to be put off like the other men who had proposed marriage. If she could only let herself trust him....

1035 IF LOVE BE BLIND Emma Goldrick
Penn Wilderman, suffering from temporary snow blindness, is convinced by her manner that Philomena Peabody, who's looking after him, is a sweet little old lady. This doesn't worry Phil, until in order to win a custody battle for his son, Penn asks Phil to marry him!

1036 DON'T ASK FOR TOMORROW Susanne McCarthy
Kate hires skipper Sean McGregor to help prove that her late husband had discovered the wreck, the *Belle Etoile*. Sean had worked with her husband, and guards a secret concerning him. But Kate soon discovers that she must give up the past—or betray her love.

1037 TANGLED HEARTS Carole Mortimer
Love, hate, loyalty all mix in Sarah's mind. She wants to run. But no matter what it costs, she can't let anyone else in her family be denied love because of Garrett Kingham—and her fear of facing him again.

1038 ELDORADO Yvonne Whittal
Gina's schoolgirl crush on Jarvis had long been replaced by a more mature emotion. She is woman enough now to know that her feelings are somehow being manipulated. And she can't help wondering if Jarvis is really interested in her—or just in her property.

Available in December wherever paperback books are sold, or through Harlequin Reader Service:

In the U.S.
901 Fuhrmann Blvd.
P.O. Box 1397
Buffalo, N.Y. 14240-1397

In Canada
P.O. Box 603
Fort Erie, Ontario
L2A 5X3

**For the millions who can't read
Give the Gift of Literacy**

One out of five adults in North America
cannot read or write well enough
to fill out a job application
or understand the directions on a bottle of medicine.

**You can change all this by joining the fight
against illiteracy.**

For more information write to:
Contact, Box 81826, Lincoln, Neb. 68501
In the United States, call toll free: 1-800-228-8813

**The only degree you need
is a degree of caring**

LIT-A-1R